CHIN
Music

CHIN MUSIC

a novel by

JAMES McMANUS

CROWN PUBLISHERS, INC.

NEW YORK

Sections of this novel have previously been published in the following: *Another Chicago Magazine, B-City, New Directions, Oink!, Syncline, TriQuarterly, Zero One* (London).

The author is grateful to the Illinois Arts Council for support while this work was in progress.

Published by Crown Publishers, Inc.,
One Park Avenue, New York, New York 10016 and simultaneously in Canada by
General Publishing Company Limited
Manufactured in the United States of America

CROWN is a trademark of Crown Publishers, Inc.

Library of Congress Cataloging in Publication Data
McManus, James.
    Chin Music.
    I. Title.
PS3563.C386C48   1985   813'.54   85-4125
ISBN 0-517-55816-5

10 9 8 7 6 5 4 3 2 1

First Edition

CHIN

Music

Aurora on in to Lake Michigan, from Half Day to Flossmoor, King Panic reigns in fast forward. Believe it. The Hawk has skipped town it's so hectic. While above the Sears Tower, on this crisp Tuesday morning of bright zero Indian summer, a chevron of mallards flies by, headed north by northwest toward the Arctic. It's strange. Traffic's impacted along Lake Shore Drive and the Kennedy, on the Ryan and Edens and Stevenson, and on 294 and the Daley—and out toward O'Hare it gets worse. The side streets are no picnic either. Down Cottage Grove, across 35th Street, up Halsted, it's one long gigantic stampede. The Magnificent Mile's a bad joke. Suicides bounce down the sides of the Hancock, finding the future in huge frantic gulps, while a single handheld Panasonic is catching the antics of gawkers. Looters and gropers are having a field day as well, getting trampled and crushed in the process, but still. And the Loop's a continuous frenzy. There's gunfire, bloodshed galore, and loud music, and countless premortem tableaux. Just believe it. For while in most other million-plus cities much north of the Tropic of Cancer it's already all but all over, in Chicago it's still just beginning.

In the end, Jesse knows, it'll all come down to a process of elimination. Always does, always will. It's the thing about being a captain that hacks him the most. Whoever gets first pick by winning the chin up also has to decide who gets picked last. The right to take Ndele or Maggie or Dougie, in other words, also forces you to say who's the dufus, the megaturd, the absolute crappiest player. God.

He holds out the upside down Aaron to Maggie, who's captaining now for Black Jesse because Black Jesse's mama came by just a couple of minutes ago in her pathetic old Olds and dragged his ass home in a hurry. Jesse's convinced that he knows what is happening, why most of the teachers have already left, and why some of the parents are frantic to pick up their kids—Leon's old man even drove his green pickup about halfway up onto the sidewalk—but he's decided he's not gonna think about that. Either that or about how his dad might be doing. At least not just yet. Too distracting. He watches the sky while deciding all this, looking for planes or bright lights, until all of a sudden he feels Maggie's fist grab the Aaron just above his, at the label. Okay. It feels kind of strange, especially the way the soft meaty part of her palm is pressing down warm on this thumb. It feels good.

He places his other (left) fist over Maggie's, Maggie places hers over his, and they stare at each other: two gawky ducklings, bony and taut, both of them much much too tall for their ages, but sturdy. And Maggie is taller, which just drives Jesse nuts, even if it's not by that much. The one girl in class doesn't make him wanna start tossing his Total and she has to go be this big gonzo sucker you gotta look up just to look at her. Jeez.

There are six inches left on the bat. Jesse lets go with his bottom hand, taking the opportunity to dry that palm off on his strides, then places a (legal) three-fingered fist upside down over Maggie's, leaving his pinkie stuck sideways like some sort of stretched-out square-root sign. All right. About half of his classmates look on with interest, galvanized even, popping their sugarless gum: at which point will *they* get selected? The rest could care less.

Maggie stares long and hard at what's left of the Aaron, gauging her tactical options: three fingers, two, or a wedgie. Is it possible she might even try for a claw now? Who knows.

Another eight seconds go by.

"Too much drama, mama," goes Jesse. Because all of a sudden he's anxious to get this thing over with. And besides. His wrist's getting tired of making this upside down fist.

Maggie at last forks a wedgie on top of his three-fingered fist.

"*Fi*nally," goes Jesse.

"I'll give you finally," goes Maggie.

"Yeah sure."

Furious extrapolation now on both of their parts,

even though the options are few. What Jesse can't figure is whether he still wants to lose, or even whether he'd ever wanted to lose in the first place. After all. Getting first ups and not having to pick second-last just might not make up for losing a chin up to Maggie, a girl and all that, front of everybody. Losing an occasional chin up to Black Jesse's one thing, but White Jesse losing to *Maggie?* Come on.

"Too much drama, mama," croaks Maggie, mocking his voice and delivery.

"Yeah yeah yeah."

"Just come on."

On the spur of the moment he decides that he'll let Maggie kick. What the heck. He shows this by letting go of the bat with his left hand and reaching down over the top with his right, clasping the nub with his fingertips.

"Eagle's claw," he announces. "Let's go."

The move causes whews, ahs, and oohs from his classmates: it's been quite a long time since White Jesse's been maneuvered into having to claw for the kick. And the one who looks shook up the most's good old Maggie. She blinks, lets go of the bat, smirks, and backs up. The rest of the kids crowd in close.

Jesse's aware that the secret in this situation is to let the bat dangle down pathetic and all, conserving the strength in your fingertips for that one last split second, then to tighten your grip up with all of your might and at the same time *just real real real gently* swing the bat up and out in the kick's same direction to help you absorb the momentum. He's decided to take

Maggie's first two best shots, see how he does, and *then* make up his mind what to do.

Maggie grunts hard as her first kick gets launched. Jesse's ready. The bat stands up straight for a second, torquing his wrist and his forearm, actually hurting in fact, threatening to pop from his fingers. Then it topples back down perpendicular.

Jesse just sighs in mock pity. *Poor Maggie.* He is, after all, the acknowledged tactical master at this sort of thing, and, while there's not all that much bat to claw onto, there's still enough left for old Jesse.

So but since Maggie had already looked pretty whupped, her second try catches Jesse off guard. Instead of kicking outward and up like on her first try, this time she gives it a quick straight karate-style chop. And it's vicious. Jesse's knuckles turn white as he tries to hold on—but somehow or other he does.

"No contest," he goes, stifling this enormous fake yawn. "I mean, it's a mismatch."

"Looks like you's shit outta luck, Faggie Maggie," goes Wanda, who as always is looking for trouble.

"You got *that* right," goes Jesse. He just can't resist. *Faggie Maggie.*

Maggie Bronx cheers him—he can actually feel the spray on his chin—then suggests that he go bag his face. It looks like she's just about to flip him off too, either that or give up and start bawling. For a second or two, he feels sorry.

What she actually does, though, is give the bat one final kick. It's a mother. (In a way this is lucky for Jesse. If she *had* given up, or just gave it a half-hearted tap, there's no way he'd've been able to tank it. But still.) The next thing he knows is the Aaron's been yanked from his fingers and he's watching it whang end over end through the air, scattering classmates, clanging off the side of the backstop, then down to the ground with a thud. He has lost!

To Jesse it feels like he's dying, even though he still can't be certain whether it was the humungous kick Maggie came up with that did it or if he'd really been able to accidentally-on-purpose let go after all. Either way, he has lost, and most of his classmates are whooping and pounding their gloves in approval. The girls in particular are hooting and partying down. Ndele and Dougie look stunned.

Jesse does his best to look pissed. It's not all that hard. At the same time, however, he tries to include in his expression at least the hint of the possibility that maybe, just maybe, he might've let go, well, on purpose. He looks over quickly at Maggie, trying to establish some eye contact, or charm her somehow, hoping she'll see things his way.

No way Maggie buys it. Besides. She's too busy anyway taking backslaps and fives from the rest of the pitiful girls. It's a nightmare. Jesse wonders if it's possible that, in her exuberance, she'd actually pick one of *them* before Ndele or Dougie or Gil.

In the meantime he also has totted the number of players still left. Counting Maggie and him, just fifteen, which means rightfield will have to be closed and they might have to play pitcher's hand. It also means that he not only loses the chin up, but he *still* has to pick second-last. Is he ready for that? He can't say. He closes his eyes for a second: is Maggie still there? He opens them up: yes she is. So okay. He fingers the pimple or two on his chin, then rubs up and down with his thumb. It makes him feel slightly less lousy to be able to hear the tickle and scratch of his small patch of flimsy blonde whiskers. Coefficient of friction, he thinks. Or something like that. He's a man.

Maggie turns back to him finally. She's ready to pick. She looks pretty proud of herself.

Jesse looks up at the sky. There's a chevron of geese flying by, headed north, but nobody's noticed but him. He feels sick.

"Dougie," goes Maggie, pounding her glove. "I take Dougie."

A dark handsome man lurches upright in bed in Room 321 of the intensive-care unit of Wesley Memorial Hospital. His neck, chest, and shoulders are sinewy, muscular. His eyes are lead blue. He's bewildered. For forty-three hours he'd lain there, out cold, but he's just raised his level of consciousness from Series IV comatose on up through stuporous, combative, agitated, and lethargic to alert but with Type C amnesia, all this in less than ten minutes. He's alive, he's awake, but his head's not in too good a shape. And he's scared. Painful braincramps, like a series of miniature aneurisms, have left him in a genuine fugue state, and his chemoreceptor trigger zones desperately need to be stimulated. Perhaps worst of all, his penis feels soft but on fire.

He focuses, blinks, looks around. There's not that much light in the room, and his rods need more time to adapt. It is also the case that both his ocular-motor and abducens nuclei are failing to track real effectively, the bottom line being that he hasn't got clue number one as to where he might be, how he got here, or why, and he can't help but wonder what's up. His entire past seems a dream of angelic young female physicians, NMR scans, violin scherzos, and blood tests; his future little more than the sickening hush you can always make out just before the bleachers collapse. He feels like a man out of time.

He sees something glint, something metallic, a play of hard light in the soft empty air. And but all of a sudden his vision is cubist somehow: fractured, remote, out of whack, with tracers and flashes off the room's walls and gadgets. And then, just as suddenly, everything's glowing bright white. Such a glow could be caused by a surge in his egocentricity bias, but this fails to explain its intensity. Formative synapses crossed up by fugue state? Renegade hadron causing a stir in some gland? ESP? Long-distance saccades with the charges reversed? Who can say. What's stranger is that the throb in his penis and impending gleam deep in his dim pixeled brain make him think that he *can* see the future. He does not understand. It's a shame.

He does not even know his own name.

Teresa stands poised and erect in her fifteen-by-twenty-foot familyroom. Having just moved a step or so sideways, she's convinced she's now dead in the center. Circumspect, scared, she is waiting. The 2.2-meter Sushiza TV screen buzzes and crackles with static while a canned-sounding voice continues to calmly announce that *This is a test. This station is conducting a test of the Emergency Broadcasting System. This is only a test.* Bending down without moving her feet, Teresa picks up the remote-control thing off the Einstein Moomjy Aberdeen Heather carpet and starts changing channels. Each station's audio portion consists of either a high-pitched test pattern or the only-a-test admonition. Each station's picture shows nothing but bright light and static. Exhausted but mesmerized, she stands there and watches and listens.

Behind where she stands, on the wall over the black Pantex couch, hangs Ed Paschke's *Gash,* an airbrushed affair, mostly in cyans and yellows, of a pubescent punk doing her darnedest to come off as bored to the max but still trés intense: no easy trick when your face is the color of a ripe avocado. To the left of the Paschke is Georges Braque's *Pitcher with Newspaper, Violin, and Matchbox (L'Indépendant),* a recently discovered 1912 oval collage. Facing the Braque on the opposite wall is *Sam's Gun on a Green Table,* Clar Monaco's rendition in fast goopy oils of a cockeyed black mongrel staring down hard at a six-shooter, apparently trying to figure out what to do with it. Beneath the Clar Monaco are four twelve-foot-long walnut shelves. The top two are both solid albums, 2012 altogether, in scrupulously alphabetical order. The third shelf holds magazines, catalogs, worstsellers, verse, and more albums, while the fourth shelf's crammed loosely with scores, wooden plaques, video cartridges, digital discs, and five plastic racks of cassettes. And in front of the window, next to a helical oak-and-ash Nagelbach sculpture, is her son's new Akai baby grand.

She finally snaps to, glancing up out of habit to check on the battery light of the First Alert smoke detector. The second she spots it, however, the glowing red point, after two years' continuous service, suddenly winks out and dies.

She breathes in and shudders, dries off her palms on her pockets, starts gnawing the tip of her ring finger.

She can't believe all this is happening.

EPISODE ONE: OUR ATHENA

Athena, our guardian angel, has more than one pitch, when she sings. She speaks with one voice, an amalgam of rhetorics. Ours. If only we'd listen we'd hear her. She knows the whole story. Just ask her. And, if we'd look, we would see her. She's not all that tall, but she's taut, with great legs, in most guises. On her neck, at the base, she often sports one or two nickel-sized hickeys, but the rest of her skin is translucent. Her chinny chin chin, in particular, is strong, deeply cleft, almost hairless. Just kidding. She also has dimples, except when she's talking, and her iron gray almond-shaped eyes are like pixels, so sensored and flashing, so chock-full of wisdom are they. They are brilliant. *She's* brilliant. Just ask her. Through mascaraed lashes both long and suggestive, she sees us. She knows us. She wants us. And, if she got half a chance, she would help us.

Jesse ends up with the Ferd on his team. Ferd the Turd. With his HARVARD ON HALSTED torn T-shirt, his retainer bar wrapped round his puss, his crooked taped-up plastic glasses. And, just like always, he's singing. Not like a normal person, either, but real high and quavery, like one of those lardassed old opera fanatics, and in some other language to boot.

y el resplandor rojo de los cohetes
las bombas reventando en el aire

The Ferd. By far and away the big brain of the class, but still this incredible wuss. Has to have somebody run for him. Has to borrow somebody's glove all the time. Has to take naps after school. Foid the Toid. Fun to punch hard in the biceps. Fun to borrow your science or math homework off of. Not fun to have on your team.

sobre la tierra de los libres
y el hogar del valiente

That's the Ferd for you, though. Always singing.

The man with the Type C amnesia is poised on the edge of his bed. Antiembolism stockings, opaque, are supporting his dangling calves. His toes touch the floor, but he still feels too weak, stiff, and dizzy to stand. Even if he could stand and walk, he wouldn't know where he should head.

A trio of electrodes cling to his pale hardened torso: one above each of his nipples, the third on the side of his waist. The angiocath inserted above his left wrist is connected by translucent tubing to an upside down bottle containing a solution of five percent dextrose, eighteen percent normal saline, and twenty milliequivalents of potassium chloride, plus a stiff dose of Decadron to hold down cerebral edema. And in order to keep tabs on his fluids, a beige Foley catheter has been run through his penis to the tiny balloon that is floating up inside his bladder. He's hurting.

He notices now that his right wrist is sporting a white plastic-coated ID bracelet. He turns it to get better light, squints, and reads it. Okay. So his name's Raymond Zajak. It does not ring a bell, but still, just the same, he is happy to know what his name is. His social security number is 342-50-3333, but his reaction to this is, so what. Much more intriguing, to him, is his six-digit birthdate. The problem is that the two final digits, the year, have been blurred by a water mark that has somehow seeped under the plastic. His birth-

day, nonetheless, is still clear. He was born in the tenth month, on the seventeenth day, nineteen something something.

He figures the best thing to do now is get to a phonebook, look up this name, and call home. The way he'd introduce himself and exactly what questions he'd ask could wait till he got to the phonebooth. (He assumes without question that he's got some sort of family out there, waiting for him to come home.) Even if nobody answered he could still take down the address, find out where it was, and then go there: not real bad logic for a guy minus most of his marbles, now is it.

He staggers and tilts, dripping piss, as he tries to stand up, then catches himself on the bed's lowered guardrail. God damn. His vestibulo-ocular senses of pitch and of yaw are both way way off, and the catheter smarts like a fucker, but he'll not be deterred. Not Raymond Zajak. No way. Clenching his fists, wincing and sweating, he gradually transfers his weight from the edge of the bed to his legs. And he stands.

He looks out the door, down the dimly lit hall, at the intensive-care nurses' main station. Deserted. He forms no opinion, however, as to whether or not this is strange. He stands there, just blinking and staring and thinking, all tubes and electrodes and muscles. (Albeit scarfree and boltless, he vaguely resembles a lean Polish version of Frankenstein.) The pitch of the light and his shorted-out brain cells continue to leave him confused. Is it morning? He's convinced that the room he is in's in a hospital, that his name's Raymond Zajak, but there's not that much else that has registered. What he wonders is, what's going on? Lulled and fondled by the magic oblivion of Type C amnesia, he has a tugging premonition that something just awful's about to go down, but to whom, why, or when he can't say. For now all he knows is he's gotta get outta this place, make it home.

He must first disconnect, so he does. The top two electrodes suck, splurt, and pop as he plucks them. It tickles. The third one falls off on its own. Next, flinching bravely, he yanks back the tape that attaches the angiocath to his wrist, *a-aa-aaa-aaaagh*, then slides out the short gleaming needle. Okay. He knows what's up next will be worse, much much worse, but he's ready. Or is he? He is. Bracing himself, breathing in, he gingerly tugs on the Foley, *but Christ!* The pain grinds his molars together, his penis sings out sostenuto, his crazed brain commands *Thou shalt stop!*

Teresa goes into her bathroom upstairs and quickly begins to undress. She has not had a shower or even a chance to change clothes since before Sunday's game, which is already—what? Almost forty-eight hours ago. She knows that it's anal compulsive to be wanting to bathe at this juncture, but still. She's convinced she could deal with all this more effectively if she just felt less tranced out and grungy.

Her body, at thirty-three years and nine months, is still lithe and taut, a teenager's really, but better, and there isn't a blemish or tan line corrupting her flushed Welsh-Slovakian skin. Her three-inch cropped hair is somewhere between brown and red: its exact hue depends on the light and how long it has gone sans shampoo. The only things wrong with her otherwise are her gnarled swollen knuckles, the rough patch of callous below her left jawline, and the pale blue half moon under each green-gray eye. She has not really slept for three days.

She gets into the shower and turns on the faucet then gasps and jigs back as the pipes clang, belch, and rumble vituperatively before retching forth bursts of brown water. Then nothing.

She gets out of the shower and turns on the tap in the sink. The chromium nozzle burps a few times, coughs up some spray, but that's all. Not even the usual drip.

Teresa just stands there. The door of the medicine cabinet hangs open to such a degree that she can't see her face in the mirror. What she sees is the shower stall's sliding translucent glass door and, in particular, the reversed silhouette of a knife-wielding wigged Norman Bates her husband had had stenciled on. As a joke.

She dries off her ankles and feet, takes a pee, then goes through the drawers in her closet and pulls out a green Cornell sweatshirt.

What she wants is for things just to go back to normal.

To normal.

ROQUE DALTON GARCÍA IS DEAD

Lucia Jones opens her legs and starts carefully soaping her labia, singing to herself about nothing, as is her custom, in melodic perfecto contralto. She scrubs her flushed face with a washcloth, then lathers her abdomen, her breasts, and her armpits. She scrubs and shaves and daydreams and sings. Then she shampoos her hair, takes a brush to her back and her feet, rinses herself thoroughly off.

Clean once again, she knocks off the singing and gets out of the shower. Two scraggly dudes in bandanas are waiting for her in the bathroom. One hands her a towel, the second puts the muzzle of an Ingram MAC–10 to her temple and tells her to put up her hands, that she's under arrest.

"For what?" demands Lucia, raising one hand.

"For the murder of José Guillermo García, Celia de la Serna, Joaquin Villalobos, José Antonio Morales Carbonel, Pilar Ternera, Roque Dalton García, Vasco 'Duende' Goncalves, Carmine Sandino, Alvaro Magaña, and José Rodolfo Viera," says the one with the gun. "And so put down that towel already, you filthy little desconocida."

"But Dalton García is already dead," counters Lucia. "I'm clean."

There's a silence.

"We know that," says the one with the gun.

Lucia is dripping, gooseflesh has risen, she shivers.

19

Both of her hands are now raised, the towel is now on the floor. There isn't a single thing she can think of to say to these guys. That she might sing for them, well, this isn't even considered.

The dude who'd handed Lucia the towel to begin with now slaps her across the face, twice, first with the back of his hand, then with the front, very hard.

"We already, know that!" he says.

The gassy silk dress on the young woman using the pay phone is, to Ray Zajak, the hysterical green of the back of a fly, but so each time she adjusts even slightly her position inside it his hardon leaps out against the flimsy blue hospital gown he's put on, poises there for a second, then arches back up toward his stomach. O God. People jostle and bump him, not apologizing, almost knocking him over in fact, as they stampede back and forth through Wesley's north lobby and corridor, shoving each other both toward and away from the doorway. One of them crosschecks him now, and his clammy left palm almost touches the thick shining braid, beige and yellow, that falls to the small of the young woman's back. O my God. It's getting harder and harder to maintain his ground in the crush while he waits for his chance at the phonebook.

"I don't close my eyes when I go to sleep, either," the young woman says, to whomever it is she is talking. "I don't."

Because of all the shrieking and cursing and grunting, however, he can't quite make out what she says next. So then prick up your ears, he tells himself. Jeez. What he'd also not mind is to grab a quick glance at her face, but so far he hasn't been able to. As soon as he starts craning one way she always turns back in the other. It's almost as though she's got eyes in the back of her head, or like it's on purpose or something. (The schizoid voices or voice in his head won't let up.) So the question becomes, should he reach in around her left hip, as discreetly and deftly as possible, and then try to sneak the huge phonebook out past her? give her a polite little tap on the shoulder and attempt to explain why he needs it? or just wait till she gets off the phone?

Somebody elbows him, hard, then again even harder, but is gone in the stampeding throng before he's got half a chance to retaliate. He begins to imagine a series of vicious reprisals but gets suddenly sidetracked when a girl with a boom box that's cranking "The Breaks" at 107 db prances by. Now more than ever, it seems, his brain is on Twilight Zone time.

And the blonde-braided woman is *still* on the phone, still shifting around in that dress, slim ankles trembling on four-inch black heels, gesturing with her shoulders and fingers to help make her point. It's a body he seems to remember. Her calves, for one thing, are smooth, lean, and tan, and the thrust of her heels have caused the two heart-shaped muscles in back to be flexed near the middle, lifting and stretching the skin in much the same way that her butt's raising up the green silk. She is not wearing nylons.

"Search me," she says, shrugging, and now that she mentions it he would very *much* like to search her. The ideal procedure, he guesses, would be for her to stand just where she is, keeping her back to him, but to lean down and forward with her palms pressed up high on the wall, and to plant those black heels about twelve inches farther apart. This would hike up the hem of the dress just past the backs of her knees, tauten its fit, and make those long jazzy wheels of hers that much more vulnerable. (He's unable to say right off the bat exactly what it is he'd be searching her for, but it would have to be something material: hard drugs, perhaps, or a weapon, a razor-sharp object say, deadly, expertly taped to her thigh, so how's he supposed to know till he's searched her?) The dress's new hemline, in any event, would officially establish the stripsearch's point of departure. He'd begin by reaching around with his right hand and grabbing her full firm left hip: this he would do just to steady her. His left hand, the more dexterous, would then be kept free to start patting her down above and beyond her right knee. Since he can't make out an elastic panty line disrupting the quadrants of silk, he infers that she's wearing those long lacy drawers that just reach the top of the thigh—a slip almost, only shorter—with the slick nylon crotch succinctly pulled up underneath. (From her clothes and her hair he can tell there's no way that she'd wear none at all, but he'd still take his time making sure.) Maybe all she'd have on were those old-fashioned white cotton briefs: absorbent, unprepossessing, ideal for the stashing of contraband. Either way, that's where the search would end up: right there in front of the mound, just inside her barely clothed singularities. Yeah. What's crucial, of course, is that it at least be conceivable to a disinterested third party, to these yahoos out here in the corridor say, that a rational person could infer that what she just said was declarative instead of uncertain, with the emphasis having fallen

23

on the first word instead of on both, and that she'd either been addressing him directly or intending that he overhear her, so that one might indeed be justified in deeming said search, if not really necessary, then at the very least in no way uncalled-for, and that his proceeding to search her is just what she'd wanted, this being all the more obvious in light of, O, say, the shrug. And besides. Once he began she would shiver.

But no. What actually happens is that she takes the receiver away from her ear and just looks at it, peering down into the holes. She thumbs the change-return button, says hello twice, listens a while, says hello, listens a little while longer. Then she hangs up the phone and just stands there.

God damn it God damn it God damn it. He can smell her perfume, he senses that now's his big chance, but there isn't a single thing he can think of to say to her. Damn.

She turns round abruptly and faces him.

"It's the end of the world!" someone shouts.

But he's baffled.

"Went dead," she says then. He does not understand. Her eyes are the color her dress is. Her lower lip's thick, energetic, and trembly, the color of cheap pink champagne. "Just went dead."

He nods, shakes his head, looks away.

"You okay?"

He nods. "You?"

She looks down and blushes. For the hardon that Zajak's forgotten's been tenting his blue cotton gown all along—and, with a vengeance, is still. He looks down now too. O my God.

"Um," he says. "Ahm."

The woman reaches down with both hands, gingerly gathers the cotton up under his balls, and starts sobbing. He gulps. She sniffles, grabs hold of his cock, gulps herself, then shivers and sobs even harder.

Good God.

Her palms, through the gown, feel cool and warm simultaneously. Firm and soft. He exhales and trembles, with violence, with ecstasy, but it nonetheless strikes him as strange that this shining-haired nymph has suddenly taken to manipulating his moonbeam in public and not a single solitary soul in the mob swirling by appears to've noticed or care. He's not really com-*plain*ing or anything. It's just that

"What's going on?"

And she stops.

"It's just that—"

"This is a hospital," she says. Then she grabs him again. "I mean, this is where people would come."

As he ponders this answer someone ferociously clips him and he and the woman are smacked up against one another. Her breasts touch his ribcage, his hardon her stomach, her thick trembly pink lips his chin. He jerks his head back, hoping his breath's not too rank: he briefly considers excusing himself but concludes that it's not really called for. Because all of a sudden the crush in the hall has expanded, exploded in fact, slamming them hard back together and lifting them both off their feet. The woman's so close he can't see her.

The next thing he knows they've been separated. Just like that. He turns to his right and watches the back of her head getting whiplashed away past the phonebooth, then hears himself croaking pathetically as a muscular shoulder gets jammed a way into his gut. There's a fist, then a hand, at his groin, then a chop to the back of his neck. He feels a hot bolt of pain in his head, but at the same time it seems like he's dreaming. He's not.

The tide in the hall changes speeds now, freezing him in place for a second or two before wrenching him sideways and forward. His hardon's half gone. Twenty-five feet up ahead he can make out a pair of revolving glass doors. One's simply shattered. Huge jagged shards extrude from the frame, but people are still pushing through. The other, intact door is log-jammed with bodies, people frantically heaving themselves clock-counterclockwise at once, getting nowhere.

As he's lurched toward these doors his legs somehow get hurled out from under him and he's catapulted a body's length forward. He winds up draped across four shrieking heads, one of which starts trying to bite him. The other three people respond with their hands, scratching and striking and gouging. He connects with a counterpunch then falls farther forward. A raptorial claw clasps his thigh. As he cocks his left arm to fight back, he sees that he's clutching a fistful of curly and shiny black hair.

It's right around now that a gap opens up just ahead

of him and, in spite of his furious efforts to latch on to somebody's person, he finds himself pitching down into it. Tilted headfirst, kicking wildly, he gets twisted and snapped perpendicular, deeper, dropping straight down, plummeting, plunging, and finally hitting the floor in an impacted, lopsided handstand. The gap closes up then and swallows him.

The racket around him is deafening now, and it's dark. What feels like a wingtip digs into his armpit, a leg he can't see knees his spine. He tries to cry out, and to work himself out of this jam, but he can't.

The bodies constrict now more tightly around him and start to move forward again. His head's gorged with blood. He is carried along, barely conscious, wedged upside down in a grinder of elbows and buttocks and knees.

He can't breathe.

Back downstairs in the kitchen, Teresa is once again trying the nurses' station of Wesley's intensive-care unit: KL5-7377. She's already got the pathetic little seven-note melody memorized she's dialed it so many damn times, but so far all she's been able to get is a busy signal or, when it does ring, no answer.

Both she and Jesse had left the intensive-care unit less than eight hours earlier, and she's starting to wish that they'd stayed. The thirty-six hours before that had been one sleepless nightmare fantasia. Teresa had talked with reporters and doctors and teammates and nurses, kept vaguely apprised of the news and the rumors, but had spent most of that time in with Ray, watching his lips or his eyes or the monitors for some sign of—what? She may as well have been kneeling down praying in the pew of some church for all the damn good it had done him. The nurses and doctors were eventually able to convince her that, while she was certainly welcome to stay, the best thing to do at that point (it was already two in the morning of her second night there) was to take Jesse home, get some sleep, then send Jesse to school in the morning and come back down by herself. In the meantime they promised to call her if there were even the slightest of changes in her husband's condition and gave her the direct number into the nurses' station in case she might have any questions.

It finally dawns on her now that the phone line is dead: no ringing, no recorded message, no dial tone: the white shaft of silence is splitting the back of her forehead. She hangs up, rechecks the number while waiting in vain for a dial tone, then starts dialing anyway. Dead. She bangs the receiver back into its cradle and curses. What's even harder to take is her quickening realization that, because of everything else that's transpired, there's simply no way any more she can get back to Wesley in person.

She runs her hands back through her oily hair, pulls on it, musses it up with a vengeance. *Stand by.* In her warm pulsing brain, wave P300 pricks up. *Excuse me. Can you tell me where I am?* Her arms drop straight down by her sides, her eyes close, her moist trembling palms open out as she zeroes in hard on the Gespensterwellen and gets set to listen. *Tonbandstimmen unbekannte Herkunft. Please stand by.* Then she turns her hands over, raises her elbows away from her waist, and just freezes.

Jesse spits. It's the bottom of the first, each team has six players left, and his is ahead one to nothing. He stares in at Maggie from his position at shortstop, pounding his glove, feeling cocky—though when Maggie stares back he looks down, smoothing the spot where he's spit.

Maggie's got herself leading off. She's torquing and stretching with the bat hooked in back of her neck, letting her wrists dangle down by her ears, her nipples protrude through her T-shirt. To make matters worse, her navel is showing beneath where her T-shirt leaves off, as well as the tops of her hips. And, when she starts taking practice cuts, the seams of her raggedy blue jeans interface hard with her helices.

It makes Jesse nervous to realize he notices. "Don't worry, Maggie," he shouts. "Girls' outs don't count."

The rest of the infield agrees, talking it up, boisterously suggesting that Maggie's whole team's overmatched. Ndele, the pitcher, starts bugging his eyes out and making these sick little sounds with his lips—which maybe is going too far, Jesse thinks.

Maggie ignores it. She swivels her hips and digs in, bouncing the bat on the plate with her left hand, shaking her right one in front of her face and her chest to stand for the sign of the cross. To Jesse now, doing these things, she looks good.

Though it's clearly a strike, she takes Ndele's first

pitch. Jeers and taunts rise up from Jesse's whole team. Even the outfielders hoot.

"Jeez, come *on!*"

"What's wrong with that one!"

Maggie just levels the bat through the strike zone as one of her teammates fires the ball back to Ndele. Too cool.

"Not *too* nervous, girl . . ."

Ndele's still shaking his head.

"Here she comes . . ."

Maggie's not nervous at all. She turns on Ndele's next pitch and tomahawks it past Jesse's glove—it just nicks the top of the web—and into left-center. Both Jesse's outfielders converge on the ball, but takes a weird hop and skips past them. Cursing himself with a vengeance, Jesse heads out to cut off the throw. What's happened just kills him. There's no way in hell he shouldn't've *had* that damn ball, and he knows it.

Meantime Maggie rounds first, keeping the whole play in front of her. By the time that Zivny, the retardo leftfielder, finally catches up with the ball, she's motoring like a mother round second, her two-foot brown braids streaming back out of her red-white-and-blue White Sox home cap.

Jesse is slapping himself hard on the thigh while he watches Zivny stop himself, turn, almost fall, then lob this pathetically feeble floater in the general direction of second. Jesse realizes he hasn't exactly got a gun himself either, but still. Hurry up and just wait's really all he can do as he watches the ball bouncing toward him. Come *on!* When it finally gets there he grabs it barehanded, drops it, picks it up, bobbles it, then wheels round to see where to throw. The rest of his team's screaming HOME!

Maggie's already hauling round third, losing her cap in the process, but it looks like a good throw will nail her. Ndele is covering home. Her turn's a shade wide, but she doesn't look back or slow down. Jesse cocks his arm, pivots, skips forward, and fires.

His relay, however, is to the first-base side of the plate, a good seven feet up the line. What's worse is that it shorthops Ndele. O God! Ndele keeps the ball in front of him though, uses both hands to grab it, then dives back headfirst toward the plate.

Maggie comes in hooksliding, gritting her teeth, arms and braids parallel, hard. There's an explosion of dust and a weak little shriek, then a curse, as Ndele puts the tag on her calf. Maggie's team all signal safe. Jesse's team, of course, are all yelling OUT!

Jesse charges the plate, trying to see whether Ndele's held onto the ball. And he has! raising it high with one hand amidst the chorus of bad faith and jive all around him. All *right!* Jesse makes a fist near his crotch now, sticks out his thumb, and starts jerking it up and down like a piston.

"She's outta there!"

"Ain't no way!"

"Lissen, you imbeciles—"

"Spare me."

"Tie goes to the runner, my man."

"I'm gone kick your miserable butt."

"Not even close though."

"You ain't gone kick shit."

"She's in there *easy.*"

"One all."

"No chingando."

"One away, folks. Batter up."

"Hey. Batter this."

By now Maggie's jumped up herself, spanked some dirt off the seat of her jeans, begged rather hotly to differ. Ndele starts grinning, then fires the ball back out to Jesse, who's smiling. Dougie hands Maggie her cap.

"Forget you guys," she goes, to nobody in particular. She's dead sure she's scored. "I mean, I was *in* there."

Jesse jerks the out sign a couple more times, just for her benefit, trying to seem just as certain. Then he flips the ball back to Ndele, raises one finger, and spits.

Scales. Skins. Letters. And hips. A possible swivel for DNA replication. On paper. There are nails, tongues, lenses, and lips: your equipment. It's fun. But what sound to be drumbeats from prehistoric caves now implode on you, boomerang, become this colossal sun swerving headon toward your chin. Pandemonium. You ask yourself what's going on, and stop reading: this long storiella of Lucia's unpleasant *blip blip*. In a flash you recall that this one woman's face was supposed to've launched a thousand windsurfing devices, or something like that, and you dive back down in and start cyssan those blushing bilabial consonants, taking up about where you left off. It's a sonnet, delicious, but it's just not the same any more. Her shivering's something, of course, but what good's it do you? When all the best visuals are collection the artist, or filmed, it just doesn't phase you no more. You simply read on. In the meantime a few sounded notes from her fiddle's plucked G-string have once again set off this vast vast ventriloquism, your gift to yourself. To yourself.

Zajak comes to on the sidewalk, curled on his side with his knees clutched in front of him, naked. There's a bruise on his shoulder, cinders dug into his hip, and three jagged fingernail tracks down the small of his back and his buttocks. He lies about midway between the southwest corner of Chicago and Seneca and what's left of the entrance to Wesley. Frenzied pedestrians make their way over, around him while he curls in their vortex and shivers. A girl in a hot pink print dress fails to step high enough, trips, and falls over, then gets up and keeps right on going. Berserk. The horns of the cars in the street don't stop honking.

The pain in his head rocks him sideways as soon as he tries to stand up. As long as he'd lain there not moving it hadn't been all that unbearable, but tilted it zaps his whole skull. Keeping it steady, moving as slowly as possible, he gradually makes it up to his feet. Two children bump him, and cramps in both thighs just about jerk him back over, but he manages to stay standing up.

He looks round for cover. The first thing he spots is a trashcan a few yards away by the curb. He staggers there, leans on the rim, then edges around counterclockwise, keeping as much of the metal between the crowd rushing past and his privates.

He is now in the sun. It feels good. The back of his neck and the lower two-thirds of both arms are deeply and evenly tanned, but the rest of him's white as a cracker—his buttocks, of course, even whiter. So now what? he wonders. Brushing the cinders from the skin on his hip doesn't work: the gleaming black nibs must be loosened and plucked one by one. It's no fun. What's worse is that lying down there on the concrete made his penis shrink up to about the thickness and length of his thumb, if he's lucky. He feels like a physical jerk.

What is unmistakably a wolf whistle, then another one, both unmistakably directed in Zajak's direction, emerge from the mob rushing by. A disgrace in his face: there's no doubt. He turns to his right and sees two—what? young men?—who have stopped in the middle of the sidewalk, forcing others to stutterstep past them, and are staring straight at him and smiling. O boy. In a sense they are twins, even though one's a foot taller and the shorter one's wearing a black leather eyepatch. Both have on green pancake makeup and sport sharply triangular hairlines shaved up and back past the tops of their ears, these to go with stiff seven-inch orange pompadours arcing out over their foreheads. Their ensembles are completed with matching black engineers' boots, miniscule BYU sweatshorts, and harnesslike leather-and-metal contraptions restraining their hairless but muscular torsos. A regular pair of real admirals, it looks like, and it's clear it was they who had whistled.

Zajak attempts to appear just as menacing: woozy and naked, with his white plastic-coated ID bracelet, it isn't real easy, believe me. He briefly considers retreating back farther around the trashcan, or at least reaching down to cover his crotch with one hand, but instead opts for standing his ground as he is, facing them sideways and glaring as hard as he can. He hopes they'll infer that they simply don't scare him, and *not* that he's anxious to continue exposing himself for their pleasure.

Doesn't work. The shorter one whistles again and both of them move two steps closer.

"Heavens!" says one. The other says, "Look at that tomahawk!"

Zajak—greathearted, godlike, and fearsome—extends them his raised middle finger in greeting. They stop.

"Don't I wish," says the tall one. His high prissy whine startles Zajak, emerging as it has from such a stubbled and ornery countenance. Weird! The other guy flips Zajak back, wagging the tip of his thick middle finger, then kisses it wetly and sucks it.

"Fuck you and the horse you rode in on," says Zajak. He's scared, but he tries not to show it.

The short guy now whips out a steak knife. "Tell me about it," he says. He is smiling. And then, out of nowhere, the taller one produces a miniature crowbar. "Yeah, tell us about it," he whines.

Even though the sidewalk is practically wall-to-wall people, not a soul seems to notice or care what is happening. There's nary a hitch in a stride or even a double take as the two men advance now on Zajak, brandishing their weapons and grinning.

"Let's go, you faggots" is the best comeback Zajak

can manage. He does not bat an eye. He is ready.

Jeez, am I? he wonders.

He's ready. He's scared, but he's ready. He's ready.

Okay. The steak knife's extended. The crowbar is cocked. They advance.

And but then there is gunfire: three quick loud bursts, like short strings of ladyfingers, followed four seconds later by denser, more sustained booms. Everyone crouches or ducks, freezing in place as reports rocket hard off the buildings. It sounds like the Fourth of July. It is not.

And then, right away, there is more: automatics, it sounds like, and maybe a sixteen- or twelve-gauge. Boom boom. The echoes, however, make it hard to say which way it's come from. It's mayhem. Still half crouched over, screaming out now all the louder, people dash madly for cover. There is none. Zajak just watches, ecstatic, while the pair of rear admirals get spun round then vanish as the two-way stampede picks up speed. He can even make out their hoarse cries as they're knocked to the sidewalk and trampled. It's great! To avoid the same fate, though, he grabs hold of the lightpole behind him and clutches it tight with both hands, then turns back around and looks on as the schizoid retreat keeps kaleiding together before him.

He's relieved the attack's been averted, but he still has enough on the ball to deduce this is no place to dawdle. Yet the only way out, as far as he's able to tell, is to cross the wide street that's behind him. There are problems, however: he's naked for one thing, the street is jammed solid with cars, and his wheels feel like styrofoam stilts. There is also the matter of the wicked retorts to those faggots that he would've come up with if he'd only had more time to think, not to mention the ass he'd've kicked if, when—*ping!*—a .22 short slug ricochets past his ear off the lightpole, zinging vibrato through his nervous and calm systems—*yikes!*—zapping his eardrum and temple, but capturing back his attention. Hot damn. Godlike and daring, with an eye no less sharp than an eagle's, he surveys the steel tide before him. Hot *damn.*

Too stiff to jump, he gingerly steps up from bumper to trunk of a battered old Fury, then onto its red vinyl top. From here he can see why the traffic's not moving and why so many drivers are honking. The street's four lanes wide, but there are seven or eight rows of cars attempting to navigate through it: three bumper-to-bumper in either direction, with two jagged rows down the middle with cars facing both ways in both. In all his born days he has never seen anything like it. As soon as a car eases forward so much as a foot, the one just behind it lurches right up on its bumper. And so on. Some of the cars don't even have drivers: they're just parked there, abandoned. At least eight or ten are on fire.

But Zajak's convinced he can make it, though the fact of the matter's, he has to. He pumps himself up and gets set. *Drip drip drip.* Pushing off from the Fury, he lands on a Saab with a sunroof. It's empty. Still feeling dizzy, he concentrates hard on selecting which roof to hit next, trying for vans when he can (they give him more options), avoiding the T-tops and ragtops and the cars next to cars that are burning. Home, Ray! he tells himself. Home! Then he grabs a quick glance at his bracelet to make sure that he's got the right name.

Raymond Zajak, he thinks. And not just some no one. No way. Crafty and greathearted conqueror of obstacle courses lighting out now for the territories, advancing buck naked across wide winedark seas of great danger, *blip blip*.

Only three or four carwidths to go. Cock and balls jouncing, the warm autumn sun on his backside, Zajak keeps zigzagging forward. A bullet zings past, pretty close, and he's heckled and booed by some drivers. Fuck *them!* A bottle explodes near his feet. He ignores it. His wheels have a good bit more spring now, and when hands reach out windows to grab him he side-steps or kicks them. Take that! The honking's begun to get deafening, but the surge of adrenaline seems to have tempered his headache. So far at least, the crossing's been—almost—fun.

A pair of young women on the opposite sidewalk have begun to take note of his rampantly leonine bod. One of them's got two fingers pressed to her tongue and is whistling, while her friend clicks away with her Canon. Mortified, Zajak turns sideways and covers his crotch with one hand, but at the same time he tries to keep going. Bad move. His timing's thrown off, and the balance he loses is crucial. Just as he's crossing from Beetle to Fiat, which is tricky enough to begin with, he—*shit!*—almost slips down between the jammed doors. He is forced to proceed crotch exposed.

But still. Almost there. The penultimate car's a Camaro or Trans-Am or something with four old blown speakers blasting raunch out its wide open windows. It's a song Zajak's heard many times but still can't quite place: quick gonzo rimshots, redundant E-minor progression, high rabid wailing, and feedback. The driver's too busy whanging air-guitar bar chords to care too much *what's* going on. Zajak steps over him, inadvertently breathing some cheap homegrown reefer, then gets set to make one final leap. *Blip blip blip.* He makes it, no problem, but he suddenly feels very strange. Not dizzy. Not stoned. Simply strange. When he finally steps down to the trunk of the burgundy Quantum buckled aginst the far curb, a half dozen women have crowded around and are cheering him, applauding the fact that he's made it. And all things considered, he feels pretty proud of himself. And he should. The catch is that inside his head now he swears he can feel something dripping.

Though she can't hardly feel it, Teresa's been clutching the car keys so hard for the last fifty seconds that one of the jaggeder, less worn-down ridges is ready to puncture her thumb. Wesley or Latin School. Husband or son. Mutually exclusive disjunctions, it looks like. Or what.

By remote-control thing from her purse she commands the garage door to open. It works. Her sweatshirt lights up for a second as she moves through a rhombus of sun in the driveway, then darkens again in the shade of their yellowing pear tree. Richmond, the raven that nests under one of their gables, caws hoarsely.

The 964, as per usual, is still in the shop: Teresa can't even remember what its problem is this time around. She gets in her old turquoise Stanza and starts it with only two tries, then right away turns on the radio. She checks both the AM and FM, still hopeful, but all she can get are some glitches and blips where the stations had been and a hum on the gaps in between.

Raymondo or Jesso. They've both gotta need her, but which one's she likely to get to? The gunshots she's heard coming from down toward the Loop really don't scare her that much, but she guesses that traffic that way would be murder. In which case a safe room and bed in Wesley's intensive-care unit might be

Mondo's best bet after all. Though the idea of not being with him that last split split second makes her go just about frantic. And but so why hasn't Jesso come *home?*

She settles back into the cool leather bucket, guns the gas, clutches, shifts into R, and just sits there. She's nervous. Her thumb hurts. She's thinking. The School'd be much closer, but—what?

She corkscrews around and, with one shaky hand on the headrest beside her, backs recklessly out onto Schiller.

Jesse's on deck, in a trance, watching Maggie, who's pitching, and thinking about where his dad is, and why, when Zivny comes up from behind him and hands him this square piece of cardboard.

He flips the thing over. "What's this?"

Zivny just squints and walks off.

He looks at the cardboard, confused. What it turns out to be is the front of a Land O Lakes margarine package, the one with the squaw squatting down with her back to a bright yellow sunrise and holding a plate with some margarine on it, or butter. Someone, however, has fashioned a rectangular flap across the chest of her beaded and fringed buckskin jerkin, just inside where her fingers are holding the plate up, then cut out her two bended knees from the very same picture on some *other* Land O Lakes package and taped them up under the flap, facing out.

Jesse's on guard as he lifts up the flap, but so, since the knees have no nipples, he just doesn't get it at first.

Lucky Zajak. The very next trashcan he comes to contains what at least damn sure *looks* like a T-shirt, and is. He fishes it out, shakes off some gum wrappers and barbequed popcorn, then holds it at arms' length before him. Voila!

It's inside out, damp, and bright orange, with three concentric rings of dried sweat at the armpits, but Zajak cannot be a chooser. It also just happens to be the Official Commemorative T-Shirt of the umpteenth anniversary of Chicago's Great Fire, but in order to appreciate the incredible beauty of this, Zajak would have to be sufficiently concerned with such matters to turn the whole thing rightside out, recognize Roger Brown's patented Imagist Loopline silkscreened in black on the front, plus be able to fathom the subtle and tricky significance of the clouds and the flames and the dates. Ain't no way. To him the thing's simply a T-shirt.

But so how do I work this? he wonders. It looks like it fits him, but donned as a regular T-shirt it would not really do him much good. He is forced to tap into his shrinking reserves of resourcefulness. Draping it down like an apron gives him maximum coverage up front, but the sleeves are too short to be pulled back around and then tied. Folding it crosswise and fitting it on as a diaper almost works too, with excellent coverage both in front and in back, but the thing is, he ain't got no pins.

He persists. After two more unviable versions—as loincloth, as codpiece—he eventually gets the idea to turn the damn thing upside down and step *into* it, right foot down throught the neckhole, left foot out through one sleeve, then hitch it back up round his waist. Well well well. It's too tight around his left thigh, but he solves this by yanking and stretching the sleeve out. Okay. No velcro? No belt? No suspenders? No problem. Because when he gathers together the bottom (now top) of the shirt, twists it tight, then knots it above his left hip, motherfucker gots his damn self a flash pair of bright orange, albeit lopsided, bloomers.

FOUND EPISODE

For the incontinent adult, isn't it time we did better?

No more diapers. Becker introduces the first fecal device for the incontinent adult. It will change the way we live.

The Becker Fecal Incontinent Collector brings more dignity and comfort to the patient than anything ever developed.

An overpromise?

Perhaps you need to see it up close to appreciate its finer points.

A ring, made of flexible, closed-cell foam to prevent the transfer of liquid.

A unique design for better contour and anatomical fit.

An easily removable, moisture-resistant adhesive.

The low-profile collector is also special. It's pleated for increased volume. Vented to allow for a temperature probe. And made with an odor barrier film.

The Becker fecal device will greatly improve your patient-care operation.

But think of the other rewards. Self-respect for the elderly. And even more important, a chance to give people, who may not have much of a future, an infinitely happier present.

Jesse swings and he misses, a first. Of all the moments so far in his life, it's the worst.

And then *Jeeeez!*

Somebody's farted humungously into the piezo-electromagnetic whirlwind or something, but Jesse says nothing.

You smelt it you dealt it.

He cocks his bat twice, shrugs away some of his nervousness, then zeroes in hard on the dark seams of Maggie's next pitch enticingly rotating toward him.

A phonebooth!

Zajak runs over, pulls out the huge black Chicago directory, starts to riffle its membrane-thin pages. He's so fired up he can't see straight.

He locates the Zs right away, but at this point the going gets tougher: the weight of the book is now so far off kilter it's hard to hold open onehanded. He turns back some pages, hits Y, flips all the way up to Zu, almost drops it. Cursing and frantic, he juggles the book back in balance, then bears down as hard as he can.

Zitz . . . Zinner . . . Zimmerman. Shit! He moistens his page-turning fingers, concentrates, zeroes in closer. He's trying to calm himself down.

Zappa . . . Zapata . . . about a half dozen Zahns . . . Zahnuzelski. More like it. He's got the right page now. Let's see. Zamora . . . Zamudo . . . (He still doesn't have all the dots on his dice, and his ability to think alphabetically isn't quite back to midseason form.) He keeps looking. There's a Zahlword . . . a Zahlwort . . . three or four Zakoffs . . . a Zaino . . . a Zaitz . . . a long row of Zajacs . . . a-a-and Zajak!

There are thirteen all told, but only one Raymond, and he thanks dear sweet Jesus for that. He looks at the name on his bracelet again, then back at the page in the phonebook:

ZAJAK Raymond 1367 N. State————UN4-3351

He doesn't have change, but concludes he can call home collect. (What name should he give to the operator? Mr. Zajak? No way. Raymond? Too formal. Ray seems the safest: just Ray.) He's strangely not nervous, but when he picks up the phone *there's no dial tone*. He presses some buttons and listens, waiting and hoping. But nope: there is nothing: just billions of miles of dead silence. He hangs up and curses, then lifts the receiver and listens again. And then curses.

The only and best thing to do, he now knows, is to go there. Since there's nothing on or with which to write the address down, and no *way* he can count on his memory, he tears the whole page from the phonebook, reads his address one more time, then folds the page up into ninths and tucks it down inside his bloomers. All set. 1367 North State Street. He's got it.

The only thing is now, where is it? Time picks up speed as he wonders. He's trying to think what to do, but he can't, and he starts to get more and more frantic. (He could ask for directions, of course, but the state that he's in helps obscure certain options that would otherwise strike him as obvious.) The phonebook now dangles from the end of its chain, and Zajak can't not watch it spin. The wasps and despair and the ragweed of autumn close in while he watches, and he almost gets stung. And he sneezes. His heart almost stops for a second. He's sweating. In panic. He sneezes again, and again, then gets stung. Fuck! *Where is it!*

Tuesday, and I'm in The Gap again, hawking straightlegged Levi's and smoking the last cigarette of my life: my pack of Lucky Strike Lights is now empty, and I've vowed never to buy another one. An attractive young woman is in one of the dressing rooms, trying on a pair of my pants, and I'm dekking her through one of the three two-way mirrors in the office, passing the time while I wait for the manager. I'm also listening to Brubeck and Mulligan *Live at the Berlin Philharmonic* on my Walkman. The manager will be back any minute with his own pack of cigarettes, so this will be my first big chance to test my resolve.

Unhappy with the first pair she tries on, the woman begins pushing the dark stiff new denim back down her thighs: it's not easy. As she struggles and shimmies, I fall somehow into a kind of half-lucid reverie: I imagine that the fate of every last person on Earth hangs on whether I can toss the empty pack of cigarettes into the wastebasket. The wastebasket is next to a file cabinet, about eight feet away: although a corner of the manager's desk blocks my view of a third of the rim, the shot is quite makable. (I'm no Larry Bird but I did play some guard and small forward in high school.) It's got to be me who makes this shot, it has to be made from where I am already standing, and it has to be made *on the first try*. All the rules governing the shot have been specified by "a UN committee assembled

51

especially for the momentous occasion." I'll be forced, for example, to stand behind a thin purple line in the blue carpet's pattern being monitored by a thin beam of light: if broken by my shoe, the light's circuit will automatically trigger the destruct mechanism. If I miss the same thing will happen: the entire planet will start disintegrating a continent at a time, according to alphabetical order, then explode into space. Africa, I realize, would be the first landmass to go then, though not by that much.

Across the polarized glass from me, the woman is casually testing the elastic in her boys' cotton undershorts and fiddling with the thin silver chain she wears looped twice around her waist (and on which, I notice, nothing is hanging). She appears to be through for the moment with the trying-on process, but not about to go anywhere or get dressed again, either. The shot, I decide, will be dedicated to her.

Sweaty palms and all, I am ready. At my personal request, "The Sermon on the Mount" has become the designated background music. My second request, for one final cigarette, has been denied by the UN committee.

Weighing the pack in my palm, I find it heavy and well balanced enough to be accurate with. Everything is set.

I breathe in deeply and shoot as I exhale, thinking *All the good luck in the world can't save it now.*

From the beginning it looks like a basket. The pack, however, manages to graze the corner of the desktop, causing it to carom about thirty degrees off its arc and fall out of sight. For a second or two, I get scared.

But the committee sees everything: they have the whole shot on videotape and will need only a few seconds more to issue their findings.

When I glance back in on her now, the woman appears to be staring me straight in the eye. Her sweater's pulled up past her breasts. With her left hand she tweaks her right nipple. Her right hand is inside her shorts. Instinctively I lower my gaze and hold in my stomach. It's weird.

The committee's findings are that my shot hadn't been as accurate as they'd hoped (I'd jerked my head back, for example, and my follow-through had been terrible), but that gravity had helped force the pack back on course. Special Earth-resources technology satellites tracking its flight had determined that wind resistance was also a factor as the pack had begun to uncrumple. It all can be seen in their slow-motion replay. In the end the pack had been able, the desktop notwithstanding, to just catch the back of the wastebasket, bounce back and forth, poise on the rim for a second, then topple back in.

The manager of The Gap returns to his office at exactly this moment.

Maggie massages her crotch with the ball of her palm, manages to stop herself for a second or two, finally can't keep from doing it. Her face is all red.

Jesse's on first. No one's called time, but he holds. He still can't figure out what he was thinking of, lining it back at the mound, and on purpose, especially with pitcher's hand out.

Maggie's still wincing, hyperventilating almost, furiously gulping back tears.

"You okay?" Jesse wonders, out loud.

There is laughter, then silence.

"Hey Maggie?"

Teresa hits the hooks, no time to downshift or back up or turn, as the gaping rear end of an enormous white garbage truck comes bearing down hard on her Stanza, whanging off chassis both parked and still moving, fishtailing out of control like only a runaway garbage truck commandeered by two drunken teenagers can, in reverse. Teresa's bad reflexes freeze her, make her cringe, make her wince, but the eye of her mind stays wide open. She'd been making a (careful) right turn onto Clark off of Schiller when all of a sudden here comes this *thing* out of nowhere, right at her, like a monster crustacean or something. And so all she can do now is stare, wholly spellbound, as it starts plowing backwards in very slow motion into her and the Mazda Ahura LC parked beside her, transferring to the orange and black subsubcompact the tigress's share of the impact but nonetheless handily managing to accordion the entire front end of her Stanza and driving the leather-wrapped steeringwheel up toward her seatbeltless chest and her face, nudging non troppo her chin and her lowermost rib before its pulsating rearwardly crunch gets expended and inertia at last can take over.

The Stanza's been totaled, but its guaranteed-shatterproof windshield hasn't (yet) shattered. What it's done is disintegrate. It hangs there exquisitely latticed, poised for one last split second in the shape of a wind-

55

shield, before it finally gives up the ghost and collapses, strewn like a neatly tossed shovelful of large uncut diamonds over dashboard, front buckets, Teresa.

"Hot damn!"

"Yeeeeeeeeeeeee *ha!*"

"Jez look what you done did!"

But Teresa's so out of it now that these crazed whoops and cries fail to register. Deafstruck and dazed, she stares through the windshield-shaped hole at the garbage truck's bumper, perusing with transfixed attention the trio of stickers it's sporting. The one on the left says MY ♡'s IN CHICAGO with a capital F crudely prefixed in red felt-tipped pen to the heart. The middle one says U.I.O.G.D. The one on the right says SATISFACTION GUARANTEED OR DOUBLE YOUR GARBAGE BACK. Teresa does not get a one.

Slurred threats and curses continue to spew from the cab of the truck—something to the effect of *hey you cunt suck my butt that's excuse the fuck right out of me*—and Teresa snaps to. She smells garbage. She's scared. She can't move.

Is she hurt? She can't tell. Her legs are jammed open and back and she's spangled all over with glass, but so far there's not any pain. She feels light.

She hears iron grind as the Stanza and truck both lurch forward, groaning and heaving and trembling. She watches the truck pull away.

Thank you, God.

Thank you.

It occurs to her now that the gas in her tank might explode, and she starts flashing back to with clear fractured detail a thing on the news where the same kind some black woman one of her kids a small boy burning trapped in a blue GLC!

She does not have to reach very far for the key, maybe six or eight inches at most, but fourteen long seconds go by before she's finally able to get her right hand to extend, grab the key, and turn the damn thing counterclockwise.

The sun's shining brightly, there's not too much wind, the barometer's at 30.09 and rising. The moon is out too, almost full. The result is that, physically, most people feel pretty good.

Not Zajak, however. The pain in his head is ferocious, sometimes so bad he can't see straight. Like now. Tough city pigeons refuse to give ground or scatter as he follows the path through Byrne Park, bewildered, half naked, and sneezing. Up ahead are the Water Tower Works and the slides and the rides and the swingsets. No children. Behind him, just over his shoulder, is the Illinois National Guard Armory Building with its forty-yard-long forty-foot-high recruitment billboard up top, featuring Uncle Sam's foreshortened index finger looming out over the involuted exodus going down in the heart of the heart of his very own soon-to-be-burning metropolis, Jim, wanting YOU.

Not Zajak, however. Too wasted. Having a name and address and some clothes makes him feel somewhat better, but he still must appear real beleaguered. For at this point, as if by some miracle, a gray-eyed, blonde-banged and -braided Guardian Angel in a scarlet beret comes up out of nowhere to help him. The first thing she does is, she cures both his sting and his hayfever (and greatly reduces his headache) with one silent snap of her fingers. Then she takes his address, gives him quick clear straightforward directions, pats his butt twice for "good luck" and squeezes it once for good measure, then disappears back into the crowd just as suddenly. And Zajak, dazed but unfazed, proceeds north by northwest toward the Hancock.

The moptopped George Beatle removes the tubular slide bar from between his crooked bicuspids and grins at the shaggy, bespectacled John Beatle. Two women faint. The power's gone out in the Grant Park Bandshell, but the Fabulous Four have agreed to continue with only acoustic guitars, regular drums, and their voices. The audience of six or eight dozen crowds closer.

The righthanded Paul Beatle nods, taps his boot, and then strums down a G-minor chord on his Martin 000, a trio of gestures combining to visibly manifest a structural rhythm to both his colleagues and audience. A triplet of subsequent rimshots by the avuncular Ringo Beatle also contribute. That the audience instantaneously recognizes the catchy descant thus inaugurated is evidenced by spirited volleys of yeahs and applause.

The Paul Beatle sings.

Maggie licks off the small beads of sweat that have formed between her chapped upper lip and her nose. She's okay.

Though she looks kind of pale, Jesse thinks. But he's glad. He'd been sort of afraid that everybody'd start going critical on *him* for what had just happened, like it was supposed to be some sort of cataclysm, even though it was obviously *her* job to get out of the way or at least get her glove up or something. Or catch it.

But still.

He catches her grabbing a glance now his way, but it's too quick to read her expression.

I mean, what an incredible dummy.

As she gets set to pitch to Ndele, Jesse just stares at her long tan left arm angling up between her brother's old A-2000 with the puffy Masters of the Universe stickers all over it and the bright yellow sleeve of her official BANANARAMA/TOUR DE FORCE/TELL THE GUYS T-shirt.

He makes believe—nothing.

Her skin.

He pretends—just forget it.

The pitch is a ball. The ball gets tossed back. Her tendons tense up when she snags it.

And it's right around now that it starts to come clean to him that

He just loves her.

Mesmerized, half up on tiptoe, Zajak is watching a stocky little Latino guy spraypainting an enormous gray mural onto the gleaming white face of the Ritz. The painter is wearing a sun-faded Cubs cap, on backwards, and is standing on top of a barstool surrounded by a cordon of two dozen cops who themselves are surrounded by a half moon of two hundred or so connoisseurs, all of them—cops included—gaping up raptly at each little wristflick and drip. But the thing that strikes Zajak as strangest is that not one of the cops makes a move to prevent the guy from (technically at least, theoretically) defacing these three pricey slabs of white marble: they are, after all, private property. It's almost as though all these cops have been officially detailed here—in spite of the traffic jams, in spite of the running gun battle going down not two blocks away—for the sole purpose of securing the rights of this little Latino guy to continue his mural in peace. Just seems weird.

The painter, for his part, has so far refused to acknowledge that anyone's watching at all. Nor does he duck, flinch, or stop when the shotgun reports come caroming off the white marble. He just shakes up his can, rattling around the little steel ball that's inside, and keeps working.

What's been painted so far looks to Zajak like an unmodulated hodgepodge of animals and gadgets and people, but even naïve Mr. Zajak can tell he's not through. Right now there's a baby in Pampers, a huge fantail pigeon, a lightbulb with arms and legs and a torso, what's either an upside down football player who's watching TV or an astronaut working some kind of console, and three naked women, one of whom is windmill-chording a Stratocaster, another of whom is being mounted from behind by a bear. The woman he's working on now is on fire.

Considering that he's only got the one can of spray-paint, no models or brushes or anything, and with just the one color, the guy's not too bad. His biggest problem seems to be that he can't quite reach far enough up on the marble to accomplish the scale that he's after, even with the stool and on tiptoe, so the figures up top are distorted. There is also the fact that he's working in such a terrible hurry. It's real hard to tell, for example, whether the woman with her mouth gaping open, the one with the bear on her back, is screaming in pain or with pleasure, and she's already started to drip onto the arm of the lightbulb beneath her.

Zajak feels torn. He is tempted to stay and keep watching but suspects that he shouldn't be hanging around here much longer. Couple more minutes, he tells himself firmly. Then home.

An official police Harley-Davidson roars to a stop just behind him. A blue-haired, wrinkly, and very well-tailored old woman—VIP it sure looks like, civilian, patron of the arts and all that—is ensconced in the sidecar clutching three cans of spraypaint. The driver dismounts, helps her climb out, then escorts her past

Zajak and into the crowd toward the painter. The Harley, still running, has been left unattended, but Zajak staves off the temptation.

His next temptation, coming hot on the heels of this last one, is a tall dark-skinned black woman in a studded black leather ensemble, sporting a neat flat-top crewcut and shouldering a Marshal M^3 blasting Miles Davis's 1958 version of "My Man's Gone Now," and who happens to be bopping along in exactly the opposite direction—east along Pearson—that Zajak's supposed to be headed.

Hot darn.

His Guardian Angel appears to him now, in his mind, blonde bangs and gray eyes and all, and proceeds to provide him with well-reasoned counsel in a Vocodered voice that is not very strong but is musical, soothing, ironical. *You've been on this road before* is the first thing she tells him. But *God* is she lovely, he's thinking. Those eyebrows. Those dimples. Some wind blows her bangs in her eyes, but she blows them back out and starts singing.

He can't hardly help but to listen.

Teresa be hurting real good. To wit: a headache, a badly bitten tongue, some whiplash, a groiner, a hyperextended left knee, a strained right Achilles, one broken toe. With two banged-up wheels out of two she doesn't know which one to favor. But she hobbles up Clark Street as bestest she can, maintaining the respectable pace, all things considered, of one mile an hour. She actually makes better time, on the average, than the cars in the street—and than *she'd*'ve been making, she sees, were it not for her little stramash.

She licks the warm blood off her teeth and keeps going.

Pizza Joint, on her right, is on fire. Her throat and her lungs and her knee and her heel are on fire. An old Plymouth Fury parked in the street is on fire. La-TanYa's Tanning Emporium, up on her left, is on fire. A parking lot's somehow on fire.

So what.

What concerns her is this: that even though it was slim enough to begin with, any chance that she'd had to make it up to the Latin School and then back down to Wesley was foreclosed when her Stanza got totaled, so the question of which of her guys most warrants her presence is moot. But there's no c'est-la-vie in her heart, no sour grapes, and no pretense either of making a virtue of what now is necessity. None. Teresa still desperately desperately wants to be with both Raymond *and* Jesse at least one more time, and she knows that she won't. So she's bitter.

And her left middle toe is just killing her.

One Monday evening, in the middle of Starsky and Hutch, a small group of young seventh-world women knocks on my door. There are six of them, their perfect skins range from very dark ocher to beige, and I am impressed. Once inside my apartment they begin to take off their bizarre and provocative costumes—all very deliberately too, an article at a time, each, I can tell, showing off as much for me as they are for their colleagues. I'm unable to stop them. Stripped down completely, they march as a unit into my livingroom, their exquisite seventh-world jewelry glistening in the bulblight.

To be on the safe side I examine their passports and take each of their fingerprints, asking them to take a seat while I enter these into the system. I also bring in three extra chairs and tell them to make themselves drinks.

When I return to the livingroom I formally introduce myself and ask the women why they are here—naked, this far from home, and all sitting crammed so tightly together on my red leather love seat.

Five "just don't know" and the sixth is obviously lying when she says they were prospecting for feldspar deposits in the neighborhood and "just decided" to drop over.

To break this impasse, one of them suggests that we try some friendly tag-team wrestling, them against me.

67

I think about this for a second, then cautiously accept. As soon as I do they're upon me.

Two incredible hours go by.

Finally it's midnight. One by one, the women begin to get up, make some excuse, and get dressed. I personally show each to the door. Each thanks me for my hospitality and gives me a peck on the cheek. Not one of them will actually leave, however, until I've firmly stamped her passport and handed over all four copies of her fingerprints.

"But how," I ask one, "did you know that I'd only made four?" As if how many I'd made could possibly make any difference.

"Special Earth-resources technology satellites," she says. "How else could one know?"

She's out the door and down half the stairs before this can really sink in. I decide to forget about it.

At last only one of the women remains. Naturally I assume she'll be wanting *her* documents too, so I go off to my safe to retrieve them. But when I get back she is gone.

All that's left is her national costume lying in a heap on the floor: a single piece of teal blue silk, three mauve polyester scarves, some unexceptional panties, and a pair of ruby high heels. I can't help picturing her walking by herself in the dark without this national costume, so I rush out into the night to return it.

All six women, however, are waiting for me in the lobby. They're now wearing identical maroon knee-socks and plaid skirts and blazers, brandishing pistols with silencers, and laughing hysterically. One of them produces a white plastic handcuff, and they place me "under arrest."

In silence now, they lead me outside, where a huge limousine is double-parked with all of its doors open. I also notice that none of the streetlights seem to be working.

"Where are we headed?" I ask, and the handcuff behind me is only drawn tighter.

Marshall Field's is on fire. Looters pour out along with the smoke through the revolving brass doors and the holes where the windows had been. Zajak slows down and starts gawking. Gets jostled, starts forward, keeps gawking. In all his born days he has never seen anything like it. Most of the looters emerge empty-handed and gasping, relieved to be outside and breathing. Zajak spots one guy, however, blithely lugging two overstuffed canvas suitcases and with a brown leather jacket dangling from between his clenched teeth. A barefoot black girl—she couldn't be more than eleven or twelve—comes out gingerly wheeling two ten-speed bikes past the naked mannequins in a display window then down through the glass on the sidewalk. Other kids are on their way *in*.

The scene now recedes as the crowd surges north up the sidewalk. Swept along by his fellow pedestrians, Zajak supposes he's happy that this time, at least, he is not being carried and is able to walk rightside up, but he's still feeling jammed, claustrophobic. Hundreds of horns are still blaring, smoke burns his eyes and his lungs, the gunshots behind him continue. And but since north's the direction he's *supposed* to be headed, there's nothing to do but press forward.

The going gets tougher as he makes his way past Lord & Taylor. There's applause up ahead, an event of some sort, and the crush headed toward it is denser, more urgent. An elderly Japanese woman, fainted or shot, collapses in a heap on the sidewalk, but no one looks back or slows down. A hee-haw siren goes off, stops, and starts screaming again, then gets joined right away by two more. Meantime a chopper tilts by overhead, circles back, disappears up beyond the next building.

Zajak keeps pressing along, moving from shade into sunlight. All he wants is to get out of this mob scene alive, make it home. But he has to admit that even as the crush he is in gets compacter, the mood of the people around him has seemed to grow less and less ornery. A woman not too far away from him is smearing on lipstick. Others are pouting or frowning or rouging themselves, making weird faces at compacts. Another is brushing her hair. A man with a handlebar mustache has hoist what looks to be his five- or six-year-old son onto his shoulders, apparently to give the kid a better angle on whatever's going down up ahead. Tall men are walking on tiptoe. There's actually a buzz in the air, something festive, almost like the feel of a crowd lining up for a playoff game or a movie. A few people seem downright jubilant.

Another two minutes of shouldering and excusing his way forward and Zajak arrives on the perimeter of all the commotion. It's a minicam crew taping interviews. Lights hum and crackle, and Zajak can feel their bright heat. He spots the reporter who's doing the interviews, but he keeps pressing closer. It's strange. He's excited. The reporter's glasses and manner and dashing gray hair are all maddeningly familiar, but Zajak cannot place his face. He pushes up closer, squinting and listening. Closer.

The reporter's cordless black mike's at the chin of a husky young woman in rollers. Her too-tight mauve T-shirt says MAKE ME LATE FOR BREAKFAST in stretched purple letters. She's sweating.

"I *know* they deserve it," she's saying. She's sobbing. Although she's built more along the lines of a nose tackle, her voice has the high plaintive twang of a cheerleader. "I know that."

The reporter nods hard, pops his gum, shakes his big head back and forth. "So but, yeah. Okay, right."

Vigorous nodding from most of the crowd. Some applause. Zajak maneuvers in closer.

The reporter: "But still."

The woman is doing her best to collect herself. "All I'm saying's," she says, "what I'm getting at's that all this here nucular business's coming along at just such a terrible terrible time now for me and my husband you know, *wherever* he is."

The reporter wants to know, "How is that?"

"Because, okay, since we just won that great big huge prize in the lottery? well, and so . . . " She starts to break down again, but nonetheless manages to hold up the stub of her ticket.

72   Ahs, oohs, and groans from the audience. A crewcut Korean man chins up an air Stradivarius and starts miming dirge molto mosso, complete with closed eyes,

a sniffle or two, and melodramatic bowing. The mini-cam operator pans quickly from ticket to fiddle.

Meantime the reporter has turned, palms up, imploringly, to a blue-suited woman in sunglasses standing in back and just to the left of the minicam: Zajak deduces she must be the program's director. His guess seems confirmed when the woman looks down at her watch, up at the sky, then starts scooping the air with her hands.

The reporter continues: "I mean, how do you mean? Because, ma'am, what you're saying's that, ah, what's embodied in a statement like that, is that now that all this—" He deftly changes hands with the mike the better to gesticulate around at the people, the buildings, the sky. "You know, will be . . . " He shrugs.

"You got it," shouts someone.

NO NO NO NOOOO moans the crowd.

"But we had all these *plans*," sobs the woman. She can just get the words out. "I mean, like we never even got the first check yet."

Boos, tsks, and jeers. Two shotguns boom in the distance. More NOs. Then a dude in a translucent shower cap steps forward, demanding to know, "What you aksin *her* fo?"

"Asking what?"

"Takes two to tango," shouts someone.

Another guy yodels, "Pardeeeee!"

A red-haired guy in a U of C sweatshirt gestures toward the reporter to indicate that *he*, at least, would like to add something intelligent. "People die you know, lady," he says, glaring at the lottery winner. "This isn't some newfangled turn-of-the-millennium malady."

Catcalls, whistles, and boos, mixed with cheers. The girl next to Zajak points out that what the guy said had rhymed, "you know, sort of," then giggles. There's laughter, more catcalls, and a pair of M-80s go off, so what the U of C guy mutters next can't be heard. People start jiving each other.

"Say, blood, what you know good?"

"Silver bullets."

"Day like any other day, Holmes, only shorter."

"Yeeeeeeeeeeeee *ha!*"

"Party hearty!"

"We ain't leavin till we're heavin!"

"No way!"

Zajak gets elbowed, then shoved. He shoves someone back but keeps watching. For from out of the crush and the jiving there emerges a bald chemotherapy patient still in her flimsy blue hospital gown. She aggressively grabs hold of the mike. "Has it ever *once* occurred to any of you that it just might be kind of con*sol*ing, what with having some *com*pany, that since all of the people you would've been *miss*ing will be dead along *with* you?"

"Forget you too, chromedome."

"Well *have* you?"

"You mean it's only just dawned on you *now?*"

"Process of elimination is all."

"Purely binary."

"It's all just a time now of matter."

The reporter now wrests back his mike. Just in time, too, for a gentleman in a gray Harris tweed to remark: "Listen, Einstein, the preferred procedure for gaining a country's attention is *not*—" But a siren close by cuts him off.

And everyone's shouting at once now, forget about waiting your turn, so it starts to get pretty chaotic. The reporter, however, continues to proffer his mike, thrusting and stabbing as genteelly as possible, recording as much as he can. Zajak's intrigued and impressed.

"We gone dance on they head!"

"Fuckin A!"

"It was frankly inevitable."

The reporter just nods in agreement. The minicam follows.

"Big possums walk late, Jack!"

"We gone tear them new asshole!"

"This is all pretty incredible."

The reporter looks like he's about to add something himself when a young Arab woman clutching a black-swaddled infant grabs his wrist and yanks the mike up to her veil. "This is all *def*inite yet?" She glances around at the minicam, the reporter, at Zajak, then up at the sky for the answer. "This is all *I* wish to know."

"I know," says the reporter, taking his wrist back and shrugging. "Who knows?"

"Not no camel jockey!" shouts someone.

"Yo mama!"

What are either large firecrackers or medium-caliber automatics go off not twenty-five yards up the block. Zajak gets goosed. He ignores it. The crowd huddles closer, expecting lots more, as reports rocket hard off the buildings. A hippie starts playing a conch shell. A girl with an eraserhead hairdo has Grassy Knoll's version of "Poison" cranked up so loud on her Walkman that it's leaking out the sides of the headphones. She's dancing. Her hipbone grinds up against Zajak as the gunshots get louder and closer.

Incredibly, in the midst of all this, the interview process continues. The reporter has now got his mike in the face of some fine brown frame, too. Zajak assumes from the looks of her that she must be a model or something, even though she's not all that tall. She looks scared.

The reporter: "Any thoughts on what's about to befall us?"

No answer. It's painfully clear, to Zajak at least, that the woman is standing here not in order to be interviewed but simply because this is where the crush has deposited her.

The reporter's undaunted. "C'mon now," he says, leering down at her wool-sweatered breasts. "There's gotta be *some*thing you want off your chest."

There is not.

"No really. Just say it."

Juju music from somewhere. Boom boom. Two
churchbells dong in the distance.

"I would prefer not to," she says finally. "Really."

As the syllable *ly* is leaving her soft thick brown lips, Zajak gets spun about halfway around by a muscular forearm and shoulder: God damn! A short compact presence goes past in a hurry behind him. He turns back around just in time to make out a thick green-sleeved arm being raised to the side of the reporter's gray head: the .44 in the hand has gone off before Zajak can separate it out of the blur. There's a flash. (A cherry-cream pie in the chops? Zajak wonders. No way. More like a teflon-coated slug in the temple.) The report, from this close, is thunderous and star-tling. Zajak cringes, jerks back, but his eyes stay wide open. He's baffled: it hasn't sunk in yet what's hap-pened. And, because of the molto strango way in which his brain is behaving, what he sees now he sees in a moony and silent slow motion:

There are bugged eyes, dropped jaws, the works. Except, oddly enough, on the face of the erstwhile in-terviewee. She's still got the same beleaguered expres-sion she had on a second ago, the only difference being that the whole left side of her head is now sporting a randomly spackled pattern of terra cotta and salmon-pink gore.

CUT TO: The minicam operator, who's kept shoot-ing too. What the guy's in the process of catching is the reporter collapsed in a heap at Zajak's bare feet with most of the top of his head gone. Zajak looks on—he is galvanized, still seeing things in slow mo-tion—as the minicam operator zooms right down in on the microphone still in the clenching and unclenching fist, pans along the right-angled arm to what's left of the head, then tilts quickly back up to the black woman's face, where the gore is beginning to drip. He holds this shot in tight close-up for 3.7 long seconds as what's just gone down starts to hit both the woman and Zajak. The woman breathes out, blinks through some brain tissue, breathes in, and screams. Zajak just blinks.

FLASH TO: King Panic reigns in fast forward as Zajak's own mental minicam pitches up out of control to just catch the back of a green vinyl windbreaker rushing at one crazy angle right out the side of his viewfinder.

WIPE TO:

From the shotgun position in an overcrowded Mustang convertible comes this shirtless lean-muscled young stud proclaiming to Teresa across two lanes of traffic that her ass is a fuckin A masterpiece. Teresa pretends not to hear him, continues her limping up Clark. Whoops, snorts, and haughty encouragements from the stud's rowdy pals all conjoin now to render uncertain the precise phraseology of his next two immodest proposals, but the gist of them's roughly as follows: that His Lowness will be much more than happy to personally smoke her hot drawers for her pronto, right this instant in fact, before it's too late—a conceit they can all get behind—or, failing that, that she'll still be afforded the once-in-a-lifetime opportunity to climb off her fucking high horse and help her sweet self to a dose of his prime DNA. His reason? The bitch has got one classy chassis. Such brazen insouciance is of course overbearing and evil, but also perhaps understandable. Boys will be boys after all, time's running short, and Teresa is truly choice stuff. Even in this Era of Athletic Buttocks, her own sassy pair, without ever having got all that much strenuous exercise, still come off most pulchritudinous, so at bottom it's kind of ironic. It must be her jeans, in the end, or her genes. Both of her parents did have pronounced, vaguely African ones, i.e. buns (as opposed to, say, O, Oriental), but neither so comely and swell as their daughter's. While the jeans she has *on,* as old Levi's will, have assumed her own hindmost convexities with a harmonic succinctness that really can't help but enhearten a hard hellbent hankering in healthy male heterosexuals to O O so slowly unzip them (the audio portion alone of this most straightforward of digital preludes could itself be made out to articulate a teasing Z-minor cantiga of uniquely onomatopoeic attack), then to yank them right down off their wearer, maybe tickle her fancy a bit, dally about in her valley while she licks your slick prick, but foremost and finally to fuck her so long and so hard as to tear her a spanking new asshole. It's dirty, it's sick, but let's face it: a neat sweetmeat seat like Teresa's in tight threadbare denim can get to you, quick. And this isn't even to mention her distracting new gait, with its tantalizing assortment of grinds, swings, and hitches, each of which serve quite advertently to further italicize the bodacious rectitude of her gluteal superdevelopment. So what can a horny boy do? The kick you get dekking a real live hot slut strutting her trick little butt down the street sure does beat jacking your thick throbbing cock to some skinflick. Now don't it. Ain't a regular guy north of Brownsville wouldn't crawl through a mile of Teresa's warm turds just to tickle and taste where they came from. No sir. It would go against natural urges—urges brought on, one might add, by Teresa's coy bumping and teasing. Guy's just supposed to ignore this boss little piece of strange poontang ja-jangling availably by in his last earthly hour? Come come now.

It's this new painterly irrealism, I guess, generates all the airbrushed cleavage lately on the Foxhard Tool Company calendar girls—or is it the opposite? The disjunction's exclusive, of course: $((x) (Pxu \supset Rya)) \vee$, I think, $((y) (Ryu \supset Pxa)) \vee$, something like that. (Ask Early Wyntgenstein here.) In any event, I'm especially fond of the one of the one in the old-fashioned azure bikini (Ms. October) advertently not fondling that enormous red pipe wrench: exposed to just freeze the drip in the foreground, it still keeps intact the mascara, the flashing brown eyes, and those ticklish goosebumpy thighs. Clap rumble rumble. Guy painted all them darned little bumps on pretty much had to be a regular guy. Least in my humble book. Clap clap clap clap. Rumble rumble.

Zajak's just danced, hopped, and stutterstepped his way through the cockeyed network of traffic on Chestnut and is in the process of congratulating himself on his prowess in street-crossing when all of a sudden his brainwaves get jounced into a whole other phase by the shattering racket of six or eight fragments of thick two-ply windowpane colliding headon with the sidewalk at 155 miles an hour. He ducks.

Blip blip blip.

He unducks and looks up. The towering crosshatched slate field of the Hancock comes looming down out of the azure, glinting and massive, right at him. He blinks and sways sideways. *Drip blip.* By the time that his eyelids pop open again *this vibrating dot that has color* has materialized against the slate field. His brain's still not used to this skewed point of view, so not much else registers yet. And but then:

It is green.

It is falling.

It is green, it is falling, but not in a very straight line.

It is falling, it looks like, toward *him.*

What it is is a man in a green Izod shirt and gray slacks adrift in the cool autumn crosswind, having just jumped from his ninety-first-floor bedroom window and currently being buffeted about rather furiously by the Venturi Effect as he bounds down the side of the building. Zajak ducks, shuts his eyes, and then cringes as the Izod's green slash keeps expanding.

Blip drip.

When he opens his eyes up it's all but all over. The chest of the Izod's exploded about twenty yards off to his left. Passersby (gawkers? looters?), some of them spackled with gore, rush toward and away from what's left of what's in it, in frantic but slow-motion panic. The head and the legs have snapped off like live He-Man parts and then caromed back up in the air. It's bizarre. The legs don't bounce far, but the McEnroe-vian sidespin that's been put on the head by the impact makes it kick back away from the Hancock in a kind of American twist, right at Zajak. It finally stops rolling some six feet from where he is standing and, still intact, spins slowly around on its cheekbone.

Zajak can't look, at least not just yet. He feels sick. When he finally manages to sort of involuntarily force himself to be a man about this and at least sneak a *glance,* his own intact head ga-ga-gargles and buzzes and humbuckles, and he grabs it and twists and starts gagging.

The head now stops turning. Sideways, its ear to the pavement, it lies there awaiting its partner, its face neither frowning nor smiling.

And inside of Zajak's he's sure he can feel something dripping.

There goes everybody," says Jesse, sort of half to himself. What he's thinking, deep down, is *Eli, Eli, lama sabachthani,* although not in exactly these words. He is pissed.

He is pissed. cause: the ballgame is over. A couple of teachers have been spreading the word that classes and homerooms and gym are all canceled, that school is dismissed, to go home. Most of the kids who're still left are reacting like early vacation has just been declared. Mitts get tossed up in the air, fives get exchanged, there are whistles and hip shakes and whoops. Maggie too. It's disgusting. They're all taking off now in several directions at once. It's pathetic. They don't even go back for their books.

He picks up the Aaron and fungoes the softball as hard and as far as he can, without aiming or caring or nothing. He watches it rise toward the Historical Society Building, watches it carry then fall, watches it smash through a window: it's so far away there's a lag between when he can see it and hear it. But nobody's watching or cares. He flings down the Aaron. He feels his eyes stinging. He's *pissed.*

What he really is desperate to know now is whether Maggie's caught on to what's up. But from the way that she's joyously booking her butt off the field, partying down with her incredibly squirrelly girlfriends, it's apparent to him she has not.

But the only way now he can find out for sure is to maybe try walking her home, even though he's promised himself about a googolplex number of times not *ever* to try such a thing. (There're a lot of things Jesse might be, but if there's one thing he's not it's not cool.) Yeah but still.

After weighing several options for seven long seconds he starts loping in Maggie's direction, keeping his head down and hating himself with a vengeance, hollering out as nonchalantly as possible for her to wait up.

This is different.

A drunken mick geek gloms onto Teresa just north of Burton. She assumes that he'll ask her for money. He doesn't. What he does is, he grabs her. He's surprisingly strong, so she's scared. Eyes popping, veins bulging, with a bubbly stream of white drool slanting across his gray chin, he thrusts his wild face into hers, coughs, clears his throat, starts to hector: "Wargate's juz, jez like an other bleedin day, only shorter."

What's worse is his breath: a wicked belligerent fume caroming off the back of her sinuses, down her hot throat. It's amazing.

"Lissen, na coupla years little all be, bezifited never not happened, believe me."

Yeah yeah yeah yeah. She sidesteps him, yanks her arm free, hurries past. She believes him.

"Jew know what I mean?"

She believes him.

Zajak stares down at the head at his feet. It's still bleeding. In his soul and his heart it has finally dawned on him what's going on, but inside his fornical vault what's left of his mind still just can't help but to wonder.

The biggest thing is, he's afraid that he might burn in Hades for sins he can't even remember: burned even by *numinous* fires *forever*—no *way* such a deal could be fair. But so how can he stave off damnation? Suppose he made one blanket act of contrition, sincerely repented for—what? For pushing his pearl in some girl he's forgotten? Besides: could a blanket repentance guarantee one's salvation? He simply has no way of telling. On the other hand, since he has to die *some* day, and since everyone else will be dead along with him, what's about to go down just might be the best of all possible ways, times, and places to buy it. What he fails to consider, of course, is the fact that if he actually knew who he was, all he had, all he had *coming*, he would probably feel a lot different. That's just the thing, though. He doesn't. Mnemonically blinded by a gauze veil of ignorance, abandoned again by his Guardian Angel, for all he knows homeless and loveless, and about to get wasted to boot, what can a poor boy conclude?

He exhales real slowly, dries his left palm on his thigh, and expectorates.

Blip.

All of a sudden, as his spit hits the sidewalk, he is (literally) engulfed by what a Parisian semiotician would describe as a volume of hardball attaque audiovisuel. Holy fuck! He hears phasers hooked up to a high hat, sees bright pulsing bodies, and blinks. Squints and winces. Still there. He's *inside* it, for Christ's sake, surrounded by luminous satin-gammed dancers, 4/4 time rimshots, battered C-minor chords, and hot lights. It's blinding, gigantic, and deafening.

What it is is the new 5-D rock hologram of Nile Mansions' incendiary chart-busting smash "Virgin Targets" featuring a translucent ten-story projection of Nile's swarthy skull with eight dozen life-sized and lithe female teenagers wearing tattered men's undershorts suspended inside it like shimmying slices of guava in a shimmering orb of brown Jell-O, all ninety-six of them frantically pulsing and jerking and writhing in clear imitation of Mansions' own patented belly d-dance of d-death, all this as old Nile himself cranks out his lyrics in ghastly Bronx undertones, hard:

> *you virgins*
> *some virgins*
> *yeah targets*
> *some targets*
> *you'll get it*
> *you got it*

no dra ha
no
no dra ha
ha
da da da
da da da
da

and fusion
con-fusion
you got it
you jerk it
you grind it
yeah grind it

though when Nile's gaping mouth finally misses a beat it is instantly clear that he's lip-syncing. And then, just as suddenly, gone. Poof. Extinguished. The power to drive all those lasers must've been sapped or cut off. Or maybe the song's simply over. In any event, Nile is gone, his consorts' flash totentanz over.

Rocked to his plimsoles by sensorium overload, Zajak just stands there, sinking from consciousness fast. His eyeballs are glassy, his heart's fibrillating, his cock's more or less detumescent. He's cold. He is physically and psychically paralyzed. Numbed. Good as dead. Then, just in time, his Guardian Angel takes over. Zajak can't see her or hear her, but this is no problem. Standing behind him, she caresses his muscular buttocks, snaps her long fingers, and presto! He feels new resolve to get home. She snaps them a second time: the existential smog he's been wandering through seems somehow less dense and forbidding. Then a third, final time, and he's fully convinced any sins he's committed were venial.

So. Having taken the morning's umpteenth philosophical mulligan, and having been tranquilized once again by the trivial, he stretches his tendons and gets himself set to cross Michigan.

Hear my song. I sing unaccompanied by any musical instrument save the invisible fires that waste my demented spirit. Sing along.

Bang a gong. Your only discomfort will be quick wasting fire, your only displeasure the passage of light. Get it on.

Yeah but still. A breeze from wonderland turns back the page, sets off this horny ventriloquism. Our Lady of Angels. Okay.

Cobalt bloom neurohumor. (Into the microwave, son.) Schizoid factoids all way way way way out of phase. What to do.

Hear my song
As I lie dead
Hear my song

A brickbat explodes through the driver's side window of a kelly green Prelude LX. Teresa just stands there and watches. The young female driver is stunned. The black kid who'd fired the brickbat now unlocks the door. The driver fights back with the brick. Doesn't work. The kid and his partner have wrested her halfway out of the car before realizing her seatbelt's still fastened. Then boom. The small of the back of one of the black kids is soaking with blood as he falls. There's an echo. A silence. The driver's hit too. There's a silence.

It's a miracle! By the time Jesse's caught up with her, Maggie's two dufus friends've both booked. So. They're alone, more or less. The one problem left's that there isn't a single thing he can think of to say to her now. Not a thing. (He's dying a googolplex deaths.) They just stand there, about six feet apart, and act dumb.

Maggie, for her part, wants to walk right up to him, and give him a great big kiss, *Mmwah!* (There's this perfume commercial? she sees it all the time on the tube, where the girl actually *does* such a thing!) Tell him that she loves him, tell him that she cares, tell him that she'll always be there. But she won't, neither of them will be in fact, so she can't.

So she doesn't.

"Good game," Jesse croaks.

"I guess so," goes Maggie.

Then silence. Dumb silence. It kills them.

"Where you goin?" goes Jesse.

"Home I guess. Nowhere," goes Maggie. "Where you goin?"

"Home?"

"Yeah."

"You're goin home now, you mean?"

"I guess so. I mean, aren't you?"

"I guess so."

More silence.

A Dalmatian puppy trots by, and Maggie goes, "Awww."

Without lifting a leg, the puppy starts pissing.

"So listen," croaks Jesse.

Crossing the Delaware side of the small concrete lawn alongside some church facing Michigan, Zajak pauses a moment to watch a fast and furious shell hustle two young Board of Trade runners are working with three miniature Reds souvenir helmets and one smiling day-glo Acushnet, paying out and collecting (mostly the latter) in Maple Leafs, ingots, and Krugerrands.

Moving on, he makes out the two final bars of Bach's St. Anne's Fugue coming from inside the church, and then some Gregorian chant. He tries to ignore them, but can't. He pulls out a platinum flask and knocks back a slug of Martell. The getup he's rocking right now features a cheap maroon sportscoat on top of his bloomers, with three huge bananas stuffed into one of the pockets, and pointed brown cowboy boots two or three sizes too small. And no socks. He also is sporting a rectangular vari-vue button, one of those look at it one way it's one thing, you know, showing a shower curtain from one angle and, from the other, a busty blonde wench dripping wet. He has fresh Type O blood on his hands.

He passes the Whitehall Hotel, parts the snarled traffic simply by wishing it parted, and crosses to the north side of Delaware, where he comes on an oily puddle with a small black stuffed dog lying face down in the middle. It's sopping and filthy, and one of its front paws is missing. Zajak's compelled for some reason to pick the dog up, but as soon as he bends down to grab it, the darn things starts barking its head off.

At the corner of Ernst Court and Delaware is what looks like a strip joint. The marquee says THE TERMINAL in unlighted neon, and the windows have black-and-white glossies of barebreasted, barebuttocked women. Zajak assumes there's a men's room, wonders if they've got any aspirin. He needs both these things very badly.

He opens the door and peers into the lobby. He hears music and voices, both loud, but it's too dark to see much. A cigarette machine, a crumpled-up bucket from Kentucky Fried Chicken, some Domes. All the way in now, he's still almost blinded by the too-sudden shortage of sunlight. As his cones do their best to adapt, a dark-suited figure appears at the end of a short narrow hallway. Extending a gray upturned palm, it advances with purpose through the din and the dim and the smoke. "Yo!" it says. "You!"

From inside the sportscoat, Zajak produces a .44 Magnum, aims it two-handed, and fires.

The figure's gray hand just explodes.

WHAT THE LIGHTNING SAID

Ya won.

Mot sucks
iron anos

raw and a

Dada
DNA

war's on. A

no-risk
custom?

No way.

Less than twenty-five yards from the Latin School, in front of the Sandburg III Supermarket, Teresa gets stopped by a quartet of gigantic bodybuilders. It's not that they stop her exactly, it's just that they take up so much of the sidewalk promenading along four abreast, pausing and flexing, engaged in what amounts to a kind of strolling sudden-death overtime posedown, that they're making it hard to get by. Teresa's dead tired now anyway, so four strolling musclemen are about as good an excuse as any, she figures, to slow down and rest for a second.

All four guys have on tan-colored Aztecgod posing trunks to go with their well-oiled tans, with their cocks and balls tucked up in cups. All four have rather small heads under neat blonde coiffures but are otherwise thoroughly glabrous, though distended by networks of veins. No tattoos. Supercut traps and abdominals, superbig legs, ceps, and pecs. (They remind her of Jesse's old He-Mans.) One guy, however, is simply immense: six-ten at least, with gargantuan thighs, no waist at all, then spreading back out into megapecs, -shoulders, and -ceps. He's hard to believe from up close. One dense pack of buttock alone looks to Teresa like it weighs more than she does. He sees that she notices now and flashes a big toothy grin down her way as she navigates past him, then tosses aside his blonde forelock and hits a flexed torquing pose that clearly is meant for her benefit.

Teresa's grossed out, but she tries not to show it, even though he and his partners all seem to be strangely harmless. And now that she's past them she can finally see Jesse's-age student-types hanging out outside the school, so as much as it hurts her to do so she steps on it.

¡Andale!

On!

1. Full frontal nudity.

2. Yeah.

3. As his rods get used to the flickering candlelight inside The Terminal, Zajak is finally able to make out dozens of bodies frantically slamming to "Calling Card, Yeah" by the Zwangcocks.

π. Lieutenant! this corpse will not stop burning!

4. Because, okay, in a fugue state like ours, the facts of the case, you know, the data, they tend to arrive serially, as discrete aesthetic units, as sweet epigraphical nothings—like quanta almost, only larger.

5. If you have a good hummer and don't throw it at least sixty percent of the time, you are doing your team and, more importantly, yourself a disservice.

6. Turn up the difficulty switch!

7. Does my smoking really bother you all *that* much?

8. There's a stage with a half dozen people on it.

9. Baker-Miller Pink and International Klein Blue tit tassels lie on the floor by the bar.

10. They look gray.

11. Coke brings your ancestors back from the dead.

12. Zajak advances like a greathearted orangeclad demigod through the dense crush of bodies and smoke toward what once must have served, in front of the stage, as a kind of miniature orchestra pit.

13. SPK, "Loco Motive," full frontal rimshot attack.

14.   Synthesis antithesis thesis: the voice in the band.

15.   Dollars damn me.

16.   Through leaden light, the enduring and patienthearted Zajak continues advancing.

17.   ⌜Cy's smoking bothers me⌝

18.   On the stage, suspended by a chain from an eyebolt in the curtainless proscenium arch, is this Honey Bear, blonde, name of Lucia, wrists cuffed together, arms yanked smartly up over her head, by the chain.

19.   She was astonished to hear that the punks never spoke, got up at two in the afternoon, and slept in their coffins.

20.   It gives Zajak galvanized pause.

21.   Lucia's sheer nylons gleam in the flickering candlelight.

22.   In the heart of the heart of this soon-to-be-burning metropolis, Zajak continues advancing.

23.   Said, like, don't nobody fuck with The Kid.

24.   Home, Raymond!

25.   Home!

26.   Although Chipman says that Cadaver and Dekker's ideas about accelerated probate, moratoria on debts, servo systems, special delivery in rear, and bank holidays are taken very seriously, private attorneys and legal researchers interviewed by *Student Lawyer* said they were unaware that such contingency plans exist in any form.

27.   Zajak's lengthening thickening tautening penis scrapes against the folded-up page in his bloomers.

28.   There is laughter.

29.   Smoldering eroticism permeates this dusky interior.

30.   Animal magnetism zings zongs and zaps off of Zajak.

31.   The length of the chain, by the way, keeps poor shoeless Lucia on tiptoe.

32.   Keeps her, you know, on her toes.

33.   Keeps her heartshaped and ravishing calf muscles flexed.

34.   Somehow manages to make her thighs even prettier.

35.   Just keep your eye on the ball.

36.   To me, Chicago is *the* most American city.

37.   The substance of all this discomfort is a mindless thing.

38.   Unable to bring himself to the point of asking where's the men's room, or does anyone have any aspirin, Zajak feigns boredom.

39.   DOES NOT COMMUTE

40.   Zajak yawns.

41.   Continuity races like dreams behind the eyes, and the words are the passage of light.

42.   Zajak wishes that everybody would stop fiddlefucking around for a second or two and tell him just what's going down.

43.   That they'd cut the assholerics.

44.   (NNM) What notoriously aggressive White Sox fireballer gets his moniker from a penetrating, high-intensity photon?

45.   Excremental bits of information, my love, in

a tactic attack or in single combat, in the end come to nothing, like us.

46. "Music for numbers, computer and voice— Reggie."

47. Men in the cities throw an imaginative forward glance, fail to read Sanscrit or Frog.

48. Did *I* ever sing? Zajak wonders.

49. What's left of Lucia's gray flannel suit, her plain white silk blouse buttoned up tight to her throat, and her lacy light blue lingerie is being methodically stripped from her by two girls with scissors.

50. Now more than ever, I could repair to my Rose Garden outhouse and pick up the dictaphone, and in twenty-five seconds seventy baby white mice would be fumigated.

51. Zajak moves closer.

52. The islands, the sea, the sirens seducing us, and Ithaca calling us home—they have all been reduced to voices within us.

53. For the rest of the priapic imagoes, the men in the cities, abreaction to the castration fantasy before the primary oral or anal cathexes are achieved can often cause the fatal *re*cathecting of the family constellation *even before* the recently expiated imagoes become *re*invested with the original infantile fixation [italics mine].

54. Zajak moves closer.

55. He do Throbbing Gristle in different voices.

56. H-bombs were going off, guided missiles were flying, I mean I can't *tell* you the sounds he was getting out of that Strat.

57.   There are two Navy pilots and three or four Air Force guys in the crowd, loving Lucia.

58.   Lucia of the chattering teeth.

59.   Of the flavicomous locks.

60.   The pert pink brown nipples.

61.   The coarse and irregular breathing.

62.   The art of pitching is the art of instilling fear.

63.   It defeats its own purpose.

64.   "Beep beep there, Orange."

65.   And how could a man go to first base and the winning run be forced in if he was dead which he should ought to of been the lucky lefthanded stiff.

66.   Because it's been estimated that the microscopic state of a gas in a Hyde Park laboratory would be altered significantly in a fraction of a second if a single picogram of matter as far away as Sirius, the Dog Star, were to be moved a distance of only one centimeter.

67.   Would you get serious.

68.   Talk is the weapon for deep penetration.

69.   Wink.

70.   Also up on the stage, a tanned and muscular white boy of thirty is wearing what are in the process of becoming, the process of becoming, a pair of assless and crotchless black spandex tights, these to go with his black engineers' boots, his Dead Kennedy Brothers TOO DRUNK TO FUCK sleeveless T-shirt, and his cleanshaven strong model's chin.

71.   In our own music the drum is a subsidiary

element, but there are records of African music in which its constructive power is paramount.

72. Seldom penetrated, White Boy's dark purple sphincter is encased by his upthrusting buttocks.

73. And therefore, in that shot, invisible.

74. There but for the grace of his Angel goes Zajak.

75. O divine destroyer of the human race! you whom I adore and from whom I expect unheard-of joys, lay on, lay on, I say, whip your slut harder, faster, imprint the marks of your savagery upon her, for she yearns to wear them.

76. PLUMBERS LAY BETTER PIPE

77. There is laughter.

78. White Boy is sporting a Colt .45 inside a hand-tooled leather holster attached by a belt to his hip and a rawhide thong to his thigh.

79. A tenured UIC professor whose principal insights this morning have been that her "menstrual blood is the color of the cover of *The Catcher in the Rye*" and that "all these aggressively ignorant rockheads deserve to die anyway" bumps up against Zajak's hard body, with the expected physiological results.

80. The only thing happens to Zajak's that inside his fornical vault the monotonous dripping continues.

81. There's a war going on around here.

82. Beware of the dogma.

83. WHY CANCEL MEGASTORE DUMP   105

84. The girls with the scissors are really just kids: one's an untamed thirteen-year-old Vietnamese ping-

pong player, exchange student, and model wearing your traditional thigh-high green patent leather boots, dangling garters, and a lacy green bra with peekaboo nipple holes; the other one's a light-skinned black fifth-grader with already upthrusting buttocks, eight or nine earrings, naked except for a powder blue T-shirt—a T-shirt on which nothing's been written!

85. Smersh zirkelonem.

86. Ladies and gentlemans, let's hear it for *Ducky a-a-and Edwina!*

87. Zajak comes to realize that all this is virtually happening.

88. Muss es sein?

89. "I thought your cock was longer than it is."

90. Lucia is nevertheless sustained at all times by the workings of her physiochemistry—and, beneath that, of her atomic and subatomic structures.

91. You never really get the whole story.

92. Listen to the light: "Where are you, sister?"

93. What's on the menu this morning?

94. Lucia's boyfriend lies on the floor of the stage, painfully hogtied with the same brand of thongs that help to secure White Boy's holster, excruciatingly gagged by his very own belt and an orange and yellow Penn tennis ball.

95. Incendiary device circle, huh?

96. Every so often the poor guy'll struggle like a burning spastic for several long seconds, or until a good swift kick from White Boy'll calm him back down.

97. Amongst the word of mouth, sextuple enten-

dre, lyrical pyrotechnics, corpse and mirror, your basic word processing, lisible invisibility, and scriptible logorrhea, to name only seven, there isn't that much of a choice, Lucia, is there?

98.   Well *is* there?

99.   Lucia's now thoroughly naked.

100.   Applause.

101.   Given breasts so substantial, her abdominal definition is simply astonishing.

102.   Supervising all this is a tall woman straight off a Lindner.

103.   Midsummer baseball feels as if it would last forever; lateseason baseball becomes quicker and terser, as if sensing its coming end, and sometimes, if we are lucky, it explodes into thrilling terminal colors, leaving bright pictures in memory to carry us through the miserable decades to come.

104.   Q × Q

105.   Lucia's boyfriend cranes his stiff neck as bestest he can the better to grab a quick glance at his young love's predicament.

106.   Vasectomy can affect my immune system, with possible development of antibodies against my own sperm, and may turn me queer.

107.   Very fittingly these fantasies usually take place when people are troubled with the stress of symbolic affairs of the everyday world, and one may wonder why—at a meeting concerning business or academic strategy—he can't shut out images from Luis Buñuel's *Belle de Jour*.

108.   White Boy cocks his middle finger hard up

against his right thumb, digitally powerbraking, forming a circle tangential to Lucia's erect but still helpless left nipple.

109. White Boy snaps his cocked finger ferociously forward, whanging the tip of Lucia's nipple with his fingernail, following through like he's kicking a fieldgoal in matchbox football, a maneuver he'd expertly executed hundreds of times back in high school.

110. Lucia feels it, and says so, but without using words.

111. My throw of triple ones has brought the Extraordinary Occurrences Chart into play!

112. White Boy does it again.

113. Lucia just looks down and watches, in manao tupapau.

114. Fascinated.

115. Letter missing?

116. REVERSE LAST TWO ENTRIES

117. White Boy does it again, and again.

118. He does it again.

119.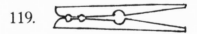

120. Lucia watches.

121. Again.

122. A gag order is officially placed by The Supervisor.

123. O, my friends, I was in ecstasies; words cannot express the wild emotion that was cindering me; without a brain like mine there is no conceiving such a thing, unless one has a brain like yours it is not to be comprehended.

124.   A woman in the audience is working the *Tribune*'s two-day-old crossword, by candlelight.

125.   A Greco-American male shambles past, holding two fingers below Zajak's nose, offering up to him their fresh cunty funk.

126.   Two Jims—who knows why.

127.   I just may have oversystematized the whole thing.

128.   I'm funny like that.

129.   Byte the Bullet.

130.   That asshole a few sections back probably thought Zajak was some sort of faggot or something, because of the bracelet and T-shirt and all, but the fact of the matter's that Zajak's *forgotten* about more prime-cut strange pussy in his lifetime than that insecure dildoe can ever *hope* to come into.

131.   So there.

132.   The poem itself must at all costs be a high-energy construct, or else.

133.   But if our aim is never to succumb to falsehood, it would be prudent to abstain from using language altogether.

134.   Aston, it just looks like all the people of this world must have a lot of noise around them to keep them from thinking about things they should remember.

135.   Am I bighearted, or do I have the word *fucker* written all over my face?

136.   The Supervisor inserts a sawed-off candy-striped straw into Lucia's left nostril and holds down her right one.

137.   Ducky neatly positions a mirror sporting a two-inch-long line of cocaine directly beneath the opposite end of the straw.

138.   Unlimited were the quantities of fuck I loosed into the mouth of my fricatrice; never in my life had I been in the throes of such disorder, such torment, such rapture.

139.   As Lucia inhales, Ducky expertly maneuvers the mirror so that as Lucia continues to toot and the line disappears, the end of the straw tracks smoothly across what is left, till it's gone.

140.   (SL)   What American League manager once defended the first-strike use of certain gamma rays by claiming that "tactical jamming systems are strictly preemptive"?

141. $(\forall y)\ [(Fa \supset (\forall x)\ Gx) \supset (Fa \supset Gy)]$:   purest blague.

142.   Lucia is gagged with a sleeve from her blouse.

143.   If some bears are male, then some bears are not.

144.   There is laughter.

145.   Using the tips of two fingers, starting just below Lucia's left elbow, The Supervisor O ever so tantalizingly traces a downward meandering path along Lucia's triceps, the exposed stretched-out flesh of her underarm, then on down the side of her ribcage.

146.   Hallelujah.

147.   Here she comes.

148.   Lucia's coked-up body English suggests she can't stand it.

149.   If one is to enjoy the thing properly, the victim in such cases must suffer, his agonies must be

hideous; while he is in their throes one frigs oneself, and how do you expect to discharge if his pain is not excruciating?

150.   The Supervisor repeats the treatment along Lucia's right side, detouring now toward the nipple.

151.   Overcome apparently by the smoldering eroticism of language, Edwina just runs off the stage.

152.   The Supervisor tweaks Lucia's right nipple for several long seconds.

153.   She pinches it viciously.

154.   Yes.

155.   Poor Lucia wimbles and wangles.

156.   That fat dumb Hawaiian jock sure plays a mean pinball.

157.   although since launch-to-target time can vary from several hours down to three or four

158.   Zajak wants to go home and he doesn't.

159.   He doesn't.

160.   To help us seek the duende there are neither crops nor discipline.

161.   The Supervisor repeats the treatment, this time using both of her hands, moving them down both sides at once, very slowly.

162.   No más.

163.   Lucia begs for the blindfold to be removed.

164.   Lucia blinks in Morse code for the gag to be removed.

165.   With the traditional melodramatic flourish, Ducky produces a pineapple from inside a tophat.

166.   This is nothing.

167.   Flesh melts and bubbles, bones char and crackle, whole bodies end up as embers.

168.   The Supervisor lights up a Lucky.

169.   The rules of Lifespan are devised so as to make the sexual patterns unpredictable.

170.   (I'm using sex here advisedly.)

171.   Zajak notices that the young woman standing beside him hasn't got anything on except for a pair of high heels and an apron with very deep pockets from which she's dispensing gratis fourpacks of some improved brand of low-tar, medium-nicotine cigarettes.

172.   It is *indeed* plausible that this observation was somehow stimulated by the sight of or smoke from the Lucky.

173.   Znamenny chants rise up, falter, die out.

174.   The preference for play was part and parcel of a Romantic rejection of the basic characteristics of Modern society; and, as in all games with balls, athletes are surrogate warriors.

175.   "I feel that my penis is really quite special."

176.   The gentleman on Zajak's left starts slapping the pockets of his rumpled seersucker suit, elbowing Ray in the process.

177.   ⟨N B R⟩ What number did Ray Zajak wear while pitching for the Toronto Blue Jays?

178.   "There's a lot of sexual implications in hitting," said Dr. Richard A. Hyman, a psychology professor at Temple University and director of the National Center for the Study of Corporal Punishment and Alternatives in Schools.

179.   From straight out of nowhere a fourpack of cigarettes is extended toward Zajak and shaken.

180.   You know that it would be untrue, you know that I would be a liar, if I were to say to you: "Zajak's from the land of Eire."

181.   Up pops a cigarette.

182.   White Boy's scapular gets sweat on the side with JC on it.

183.   Lucky Strike Light.

184.   The gentleman in the seersucker suit now whips out his Zippo.

185.   Following a directive of The Supervisor's, White Boy fastens a green plastic clothespin on to each of Lucia's pert nipples, causing her to gasp and cry out, then chucks her a playful right cross on the chin.

186.   For the third time in the last seven years, Zajak smokes.

187.   The Supervisor produces the traditional riding crop.

188.   No.

189.   Zajak feels dizzy with pleasure.

190.   GARBAGE IN, GARBAGE OUT

191.   There is laughter.

192.   Ducky brandishes what's become the traditional pineapple.

193.   A long thin formation, a Barber's Tree, could be stretched to any length, and a Cheshire Cat vanished on every sixth move, leaving only a string of small countries behind in the form of a grin.

194.　Referring obliquely to the pair of green clothespins, Lucia protests she can't stand it.

195.　Zajak's big bowel grows increasingly militant.

196.　(x)(Pxu ⊃ Qux) ⊃ ■(x)Px ⊃ (x)Qux■ L.S.M.F.T.

197.　Zajak's erection subsides for a moment.

198.　The Supervisor samples Lucia's wet little snatch with her ring finger, pronounces it fresh jambalaya.

199.　Don't look here: the joke's in your hand.

200.　She's just flat bringing it up there.

201.　Just hold it's what Zajak is thinking.

202.　Nile Mansions' cover of "Talk Talk" comes on.

203.　Lucia requests that the gag be removed, or the clothespins at least, if only just for a second, O please.

204.　The complete absence, you know, of concertina wire.

205.　All this from the girl who just the other day had on a T-shirt announcing BODY BY NAUTILUS in bold scarlet letters.

206.　

207.　The Supervisor's steely gray nylons are all but invisible to the naked eye of the beholder.

208.　You know, for a President's daughter, she's got a really great ass.

209.　A woman starts humming the boss cello riffs from the "Ghost" trio's opening movement.

210.   Acting on his own initiative this time (he got a mind of his own, yeah, and he use it mighty fine), White Boy removes the clothespin from Lucia's right nipple and uses it to fasten her nostrils together, then cups his hand over her mouth.

211.   Bitch cannot breathe.

212.   The war between the pitcher and the batter for control of the plate (more precisely, for the outside three or four inches of the plate) is the true center of the game, and the pitcher's best weapon in that unending contest is a whistling fastball up and in, close to the body or under the chin, that will make the batsman give ground—in his mind or in the batter's box—when the next pitch arrives.

213.   Cigarette Vendor takes out monogrammed platinum compact, makes herself up.

214.   Since he's barefoot, Zajak can now only wonder what he's to do with his butt.

215.   His erection subsides even further.

216.   Communists and capitalists alike are dying to get into Colon Cemetery.

217.   Zajak spots hallway off left, hopes leads to men's room.

218.   Standing alongside of Lucia but facing in the opposite direction, The Supervisor hooks her left boot inside Lucia's left ankle and forces it six inches outward.

219.   The slut.

220.   Fiddlefucking cheap little dick holster.

221.   Sixty-nine percent of the audience gots a love jones for Lucia.

222. It's become harder and harder to stimulate lust through the visual media or even via audience participation.

223. Words once again have become the prerequisite virus.

224. Even existentialist philosophers appoint literary executors.

225. Lucia makes a purfling noise through her sound hole.

226. White Boy positions himself on the other side of Lucia, in front of but perpendicular to her, and uses *his* left boot to spread out her other leg.

227. Do not despair, one of the dickfors was saved; do not presume, one of the dickfors was damned.

228. Everyone in Paradise carries a gun.

229. White Boy replaces the clothespin on the tender, delicate tip of Lucia's right nipple.

230. This is a lesson for all you young players out there.

231. Holding a pregnant cylindrical fart back (he's a pretty decent chap, I must say), his eyes still riveted to the stage, Zajak shoulders and excuses his way through the audience toward what he desperately hopes is the men's room.

232. White Boy jolts Lucia with imaginary oscillators and short rod antennae—with a kind of air theremin, then.

233. The main first-world whizzes are all pitching in to protect us, so what are you worried about?

234. The Supervisor offers a fatal counterexample to the claim that sex is all mental—or does she?

235.	Ducky hands White Boy the pineapple.

236.	Zajak has now passed *beyond psychology*.

237.	His left hand is under her head, and his right hand shall embrace her.

238.	Mr. Zajak's ball has the sort of pace and nip against which it is difficult to play a very handsome stroke, particularly on such a lively wicket as this one.

239.	The intense excitement under which he was labouring betrayed itself when he began to rhythmically beat on the top of my head with his fists.

240.	No really, do you think I'm sick?

241.	DEATH STAR DUE—IN 15 MILLION YEARS

242.	Following the express wishes of The Supervisor, Ducky gives unto Lucia's succulent labia the wet gift of tongues.

243.	O, you shouldn't have.

244.	For *me?*

245.	in that the sum total strangeness of strange is estimated to be minus one

246.	Come, come on in.

247.	Only Lucia's big toes can now touch the floor.

248.	Ducky stops.

249.	Kick out the jamfs, fatherfucker!

250.	In no uncertain terms, The Supervisor accuses our Lucia of having consistently waxed pornosophical at parties, of being a selfish little clit, a shameless flirt, a closet ecdysiast, of having been whimpering for a whipping all week.

251.	Meantime, White Boy massages Lucia's sopping labia majora with the rough outer husk of the pineapple.

252.

CALL KL 5-1791
For Sheila's Sensational
Shlong Slurping Service
☺ Sucking With a Smile ☺

in the end
the way you live
is equal to the head
you give
Why are you writing?
Don't write!

Confucius say baseball is funny game/
(How come man walk with four balls?)

It's now all a Time of just matter.
(chatter chatter chatter chatter...)

Billy Toffinetti has 10 inches mmm
of hot Italian sausage
Call 555-7695

And the light shineth in darkness.
and the dark comprehended it not

She who writes on shithouse walls   mimesis
rolls her shit in little balls. — suitable occupation
She who reads these words of wit
Eats those little balls of shit.

4Q

sorry, I can't read.

BLOODY BATTLE IN AFFGHANISTAN.
PLAYOFF'S SIXTH GAME WON BY ZAJAK
NOW THIS

Rockwell
or don't rock
at all

C'mon baby\
Do the Clytemnaestra

M	X
O	O
S	X

INSANE
UNKNOWNS
cruise

Why do niggers wear baseball caps?
(So birds can't shit on their lips.)

does Lucille Ball?
NATALIE WOOD
Nellie Fuchs
DOES JANE BYRNE?
Elaine May

let Dag Hudson
tune your piano
555-8449

You choke on it, clit licker.
FUCK YORSELF WITH A FORK!

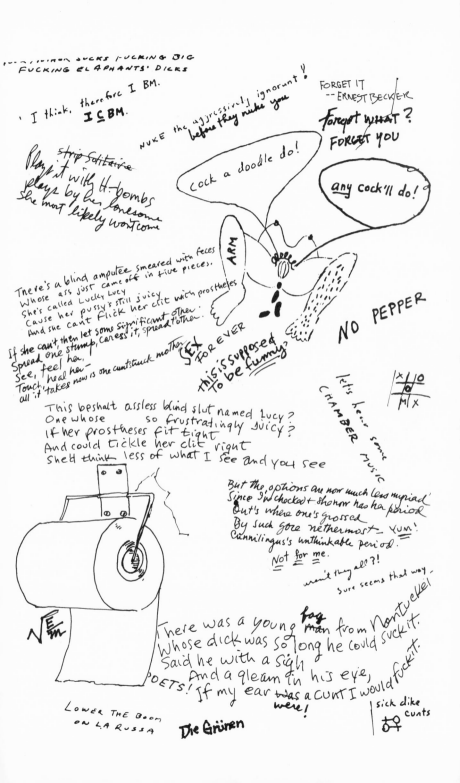

253. Hendrix, "The Star-Spangled Banner," ff, con brio.

254. The Supervisor runs the riding crop up and down—*O!*—up and down along the inside of Lucia's left thigh.

255. Spouting nodes of vituperation, the Coneheads piled into their custom RV and drove off in a furious huff, spraying gravel back at us and flipping us off in their cracked sideview mirror.

256. Zajak's relieved.

257. Jamestown, Lefty, Jimi the H, posthep griot and wah-wah chronic'ler of sundry liminoid phenomena, what say you subject the strictly metaphorical strapless evening gown of this here luscious white frame to some ultra-skeptical, axe-grinding stress analysis.

258. Ducky removes the clothespin from Lucia's right nipple and fastens it onto her own.

259. There is laughter.

260. The readers' reports, including my own, were glowing—"unusual, highly innovative, original, psychologically serious, a thriller in plot," etc.—but, I'm sorry to say, I just can't get an acceptance here at this time.

261. The Supervisor tickles Lucia's perineum with the cool leather tip of the crop.

262. A tad of catch music might fit in here rather nicely, what?

263. Throes are the only trouble, I must be on my guard against throes.

264. You'll just have to make do, I guess, at least

for the time being, with the leaping syntax but limited vocabulary of luv.

265.   Using, for the time being, only the inside of his wrist and his palm, White Boy starts stroking his dong.

266.   Lucia's two comely buttocks do clench together when The Supervisor suddenly cuts through the air with the crop, but they return to convexity and separate when Lucia realizes—*whew!*—that the whole thing was only a tease.

267.   Only to clench once again when the crop's used instead to insistently coax open her anus.

268.   ⓖ This Syrian capital is reputed to be the oldest continuously existing city in the world.

269.   The manager of The Gap has just found the crumpled-up pack of Lucky Strike Lights lying on the rug by his wastebasket.

270.   On strict orders from The Supervisor, Ducky pays lip service to Lucia's warm asshole.

271.   Gamma Ray Zajak is back!

272.   REDS MAKE ARMS TALK PITCH

273.   You've gotta protect your own hitters.

274.   Holding the crop with her teeth, The Supervisor reaches between Lucia's spread thighs from behind and starts to whip up the traditional lather or sauce, you know, the one consisting of residue and sweat from the anus, third- or fourth-party saliva, the thin slick film of whatever from along the perineum, and plain old hot pussy juice.

275.   "Noam's smoking bothers me."

276.   Stick it in his ear!

277.   In the Gauguin prototype, the primitivizing representation of a Polynesian model and the sophisticated evocation of a decadent mood are indissolubly fused in a series of musical images of daydreamlike whimsicality.

278.   White Boy torques the pips of the pineapple up against poor Lucia's clitoris; she's helpless to stave off his thrusts.

279.   The Supervisor administers three quick cuts with the crop to Lucia's clenched buttocks, watches her,

280.   pregnant pause

281.   administers five or six more.

282.   Zajak watches.

283.   Lucia moans, turns back her head

284.   syntonic comma

285.   gasps, and cries out.

286.   Zajak watches.

287.   In a market economy, pain can be most profitably understood as a kind of vaccination against death.

288.   The question becomes: Will it take?

289.   With the rind of the pineapple, as hard as he can and as nastily, White Boy phases and flanges Lucia's defenseless and delicate gash.

290.   The Supervisor does *her* part with lash after lash.

291.   Reamed, steamed, and drycleaned is what Lucia's now getting, I'd say.

292.   Her flesh looks electric.

293.   She trembles and sweats.

294.　It's delicious.

295.　It's wicked.

296.　Has the Estrogen Kid herself ever wanted a cock up her cunt quite so badly?

297.　Four more sidearm deliveries arrive on Lucia's already crosshatched and crimson rear end, six on the backs of her thighs, five more on other spots.

298.　Since Zajak isn't part of the solution . . .

299.　Ducky starts fondling White Boy's medium-sized red and blue shlong.

300.　A red-headed feminist spits now on White Boy.

301.　Lucia's boyfriend's hands must've turned purple by now.

302.　The feeling is growing deep within the cruel heart of hearts of The Supervisor that without that much trouble she'd be able to administer lashings of Lucia's fresh flesh just about all the livelong day, now and forever, Amen.

303.　Zajak snorts.

304.　A crowd of people turned and stared.

305.　They'd seen his face before.

306.　The bird what gobbed on White Boy has whipped up untold consternation, an assemblage of pique and arousal, the smell of her own burning hair.

307.　Finding Ducky's fondling inexpert, White Boy stiffarms her off of him, viciously kicks her, then proceeds with the job on his own.

308.　He's already blown the ball dead.

309.　O.

310.　O O O O O.

311. The Supervisor, by the way, has for the past seven years been a data processor at the Foxhard Tool Company, Suite 16, 869 Wacker Drive.

312. While in New York City, at this very second, the sentence is in fact carried out.

313. The sentence is executed.

314. Period.

315. Ouch, too, is a one-word sentence which a person may volunteer from time to time by way of laconic comment on the passing show.

316. Ducky exits stage right as White Boy draws out his Colt.

317. The Supervisor continues to alternately slash and caress Lucia's thighs, hips, and breasts.

318. (Meanwhile the Knight of Faith is threatening to slash and caress your very own invisible swanthroat.)

319. White Boy half kneels and half squats on the neck of Lucia's cruelly trussed boyfriend, grinding his (the boyfriend's) weak chin against the stage floor, squashing hell out of the poor young guy's personhood too, in the process.

320. In the command mode, Wylbur obeys your commands.

321. Mum's the word.

322. Because the throes of passion just *aren't* a foolproof deterrent, as witness White Boy pumping his left hand full throttle to jack himself off, his right hand to reach round behind himself with the tip of the Colt and diddle his very own asshole.

323.   Just between you and me.

324.   There is laughter.

325.   That a syntactical series can swoop and leap like a mother and still retain deep intact structure is a notion that continues to be vigorously resisted by 72.7 percent of our full and associate professors.

326.   White Boy inserts the tip of the barrel twelve-seventeenths of an inch up (down?) his rectum.

327.   Don't panic.

328.   White Boy continues to whang his tall corporal with gusto.

329.   The Supervisor watches this, mesmerized, smoking.

330.   The Human League's amateurhour version of "AAA" comes on—then gets switched right back off.

331.   The Supervisor gives Lucia a drag.

332.   White Boy's left fist is just flying.

333.   Lucia starts coughing.

334.   There is laughter.

335.   Wang Chung, "Blow the Light," hard (it's better than it sounds).

336.   When Lucia wants a second drag, though, The Supervisor flatly refuses.

337.   There is laughter.

338.   White Boy groans, starts coming, and fires.

339.   His bloodshot blue eyes rem like spastics', like people's who're dreaming they're dying or something, but worse, as he comes onto Lucia's right thigh.

340.   There's applause.

341.   White Boy is shivering hard as he storms the Reality Studio: *whew!*

342.   Zajak's not even on this planet as far as his fast ball's concerned.

343.   White Boy's wet gore is simply all over the place.

344.   But you sit on his smoke and he burns you all night with his screwgie.

345.   There are two, count em, two cases of Spontaneous Human Combustion in the audience now.

346.   Lucia's poor boyfriend's confused, his chin is still sore, he's unable to feel either hand.

347.   White Boy's convulsed on the floor, self-abused to the max, but he still has that Colt in his hand.

348.   A guy in the audience blurts out something along the lines of God, if you could just get a videotape of something like this.

349.   MINUTES TO GO

350.   Meantime White Boy is spasmodically trying to drag the Colt up to his head in order to finish the job off.

351.   Another guy hollers back that there ain't enough light.

352.   The Supervisor is staring at Zajak, like she knows him or something, or worse.

353.   You know, to be able to shoot.

354.   For the first time in eight or ten years, Lucia prays.

355.   Zajak notices that White Boy's still shivering, hard.

356.   Your noise reduction isn't usually added until the penultimate mix.

357.   It's not the bullet with his name on it that Zajak is worried about, it's the one that says *To whom it may concern.*

358.   White Boy refuses to die.

359.   Somebody's beeper goes off.

360.   There is laughter.

Jimmy Piersall and Joseph L. Cardinal Bernadin are standing near the corner of Madison and Jefferson, staring at the latticed reflection of Oldenburg's *Batcolumn* in the Social Security Building's mirrored south face. The Lookingglass Plane flies by 47,500 feet overhead. Both men wear navy blue Sox caps to cover their bald spots. Both have their hands in their pockets.

"I *know* they've got overhead problems," says Piersall. "But still."

Their conversation, however, already twelve minutes old, has apparently reached one more impasse. The cardinal looks sad. A wino walks by. Very sad.

"Hey, Bernadino," says Piersall. The heavily sedated excenterfielder's still totally animated. "Why are Catholics all the world over eternally grateful that Jesus was crucified, you know, stead of stoned Him to death?"

The Albert Einstein Peace Prize–winning vicar just looks at him, his pious magnanimous eyes enlarged by his trifocal lenses. And shrugs.

Six seconds pass. The cardinal's Chicano chauffeur stands by by the curb. He looks bored.

"I really don't know," says the cardinal. He takes off his cap.

So does Piersall.

"I give up," says the cardinal.

"Because it's a heck of a lot easier," says Piersall,

128

excited, "to go like this—" and he makes a big sign of the cross, "than like this—" and starts punching himself, using both fists, in the forehead.

The cardinal cracks up. The sun shines down on his face through the *Batcolumn*'s Cor-Ten steel lattices. The cardinal just laughs, laughs, and laughs.

Piersall looks pleased. A wino runs by. The cardinal's chauffeur makes an enormous production out of pushing his cuff back to look at his watch. It is time.

"What did you say your ERA was, son?" says the cardinal, enunciating as clearly as possible given the fact he's still laughing and is punching himself in the forehead. "Thirty-seven or something?"

"That was my *num*ber," says Piersall. He's hurt. "Jesus Christ."

A wino flies by.

"Right," says the cardinal. He composes himself. His triple-parked limousine gleams in the sunlight. "What, back in Cleveland?"

"You got it," says Piersall. "And coming up against some of them guys back in those days was *no-o-o* picnic."

The cardinal looks up at the sky. So does Piersall. So does the cardinal's chauffeur.

"No," says the cardinal. He blinks, smiles, and nods. "I rather imagine it wasn't."

What's left of the Latin School's crack Class A State Champion drill team is executing some kraftig and schnell Double Dutch on the corner of Clark and North Avenue. Teresa limps past them for the fourth or fifth time, keeping her eyes peeled for Jesse, asking around for him, fretting. She's feeling just short of delirious, like she's ready to faint from anxiety, which is not even to mention the pain she is in, or the fear. She's been hearing things too. Three or four voices that whisper chaotic hexameter: murderous, horn-blaring, brake-screeching traffic: syncopated clapping and stamping of sneakers: Stravinsky. Her heartbeats are way out of time.

Where is Jesse!

She can picture her son's immolation. His bright hair on fire, both nostrils flaring, mouth wrenched wide open in agony. Then it plays itself back in slow motion. Teresa can see that he needs her, he wants her, but the vision includes only Jesse, alone and on fire, without her.

Where is he!

And then there is further combustion. She can actually smell burning hair. His liquified eyeballs run down his bubbling cheeks, accompanied by the honking and screeching, the clapping and stamping, the Slovakian power chords from *Le Sacre du Printemps* going on inside her head. She really can't shake it.

Can't take it. She's frantic. And meantime her Jesso continues to burn and to burn.

Zivny comes up from behind her and puts his soft hand on her shoulder. She jumps.

"You have come for your son?"

She musters up just enough poise to nod yes.

Zivny squints.

"Yes," she says. "Yes!"

Zivny points east on North Avenue.

EXTERIOR. Ernst Court. Day.

ZAJAK emerges from the back alley door of
The Terminal. Because of the dazzle and
glare of the sun, his eyes are just slits.
Shading them now with his wrist, he heads
north in a sinewy stagger.

He hears music. Twenty-five yards up
ahead, in the shade of Theresa's side entrance, two blind black old HARP PLAYERS
are collaborating on a 4/4 time blues. A
couple of doowahs get smeared to a triplet,
fluttertongued passing notes get slurred,
whipped, and scooped.

Listening, ZAJAK proceeds up Ernst
Court.

From behind ZAJAK now comes a furious
clicking. He turns.

POV: Two ten-speed bikes, one ridden, one
guided by the same twelve-year-old BOY,
are bearing down hard from behind.

ZAJAK jumps one way, the BOY and his
bikes swerve the same way, they crash.

BOY: Sheesh.

ZAJAK: Jesus Christ!

BOY: Boy, sorry, mister.

> ZAJAK looks hard at the BOY, sees it's not worth getting mad. The BOY is wearing a red Fila warmup with the tags still attached and a red-and-blue White Sox road cap.

BOY: You okay? . . . Because, I mean, sorry.

ZAJAK: Yeah yeah.

> The BOY does a doubletake as they start to help each other up.

BOY: Hey! . . . Gamma Ray!

> Pause.

ZAJAK: Huh?

BOY: You're . . . sheesh! It's Gamma Ray Zajak!

> They're both standing up now, each holding onto a bike. ZAJAK looks down at his bracelet.

BOY: You know, I *thought* it was you . . . I mean, what're you doing out the hospital anyways? . . . How's your head?

ZAJAK: My head? (*It's his knee that was skinned in their crash.*)

BOY (*Now uncertain*): You *are* Raymond Zajak, ain't you?

Pause.

ZAJAK: Of course I am, son.

Pause.

BOY: Well?

Long pause. The HARP PLAYERS' slow blues continues.

ZAJAK: It's my head. (*He touches the top with his thumb.*) I really can't remember a thing about, you know, anything.

BOY (*Suddenly remembering something*): Yeah that's right!

ZAJAK's face. He's confused.

BOY'S VOICE: They talked about that on the news, said all about your temple and cat skins and stuff.... You seem okay now though it looks like.

ZAJAK: You mean, what happened to me made the *news?*

BOY: *Heck* yeah. You kidding?

A siren goes off a half block away. ZAJAK winces.

A rat flashes past, hugging the bricks, then disappears into a crack.

ZAJAK: What did you say my name was again?

BOY: Your *name?*

ZAJAK (*Impatient*): What's it you called me just now?

BOY (*Shrugs, confused*): Mr. Zajak, I guess.

ZAJAK: No no no no—

BOY: No?

ZAJAK: You know . . .

BOY: What'd I *call* you?

ZAJAK: Right. Something about, something gamma.

Long pause. They look at each other.

BOY: Mister, you're Gamma Ray Zajak. . . . I mean, ain't you? (*The* BOY *fishes around inside his warmup and produces what turns out to be the Official Chicago White Sox World Series Program.*) Lookee here. (*He hands the thing over to* ZAJAK.) I just got your autograph Sunday.

The program. Somebody's autograph is indeed scrawled down the side in red felt-tipped pen.

ZAJAK turns the program sideways and reads it.

CLOSE-UP on the autograph: a mean streak of nervous, virtually indistinguishable waves extending left to right from what can only be a capital *R*, but interrupted by neither a downward loop for a *y* or an upward loop for a *d* (you can't tell if it's Raymond or Ray) followed by what's clearly a capital *Z* slashed European style and a *j* dotted about two inches off to the right of the rest of the letters.

BOY'S VOICE: Remember?

ZAJAK's face. He does and he doesn't.

FLASHBACK. Two days ago. Comiskey Park. Day.

A lowering sky, gray as iron, over the greens of the outfield and stands. Red-white-and-blue World Series bunting. 56,651 fans.

TV cameras galore. The NBC Sports banner. Wind. The Goodyear Blimp drifts by overhead. WINNING UGLY banners get waved.

BOY'S VOICE (*Vague echo*): Gamma Rays, man. Baddest fastballs in baseball.

Dozens of fans, mostly kids, frantically holding out pads, pens, and programs.

The BOY, in the first row of boxes, extending his program to ZAJAK.

BOY'S VOICE: Not since, what? '59?

ZAJAK'S left hand, scribbling his name on the program.

Blip blip.

The entire crowd comes to its feet.

POV home-plate camera: ZAJAK, in White Sox home uniform (No. 30) watching himself watching himself on Diamondvision while moving his lips out of sync with the baritone voice of Igor Mullova which is singing "The Star-Spangled Banner."

END OF FLASHBACK

ZAJAK'S face, in the present. Confused.

BOY'S VOICE: . . . and so then, when Dimona leads off with the homer, Marietta starts throwing at heads. (*ZAJAK attempts to remember.*) Remember?

ZAJAK: Sort of. Yeah . . . sort of.

FLASHBACK. Comiskey Park. Day.

A White Sox batter jerking away from a high inside fastball.

Another one twisting and falling and ducking.

BOY'S VOICE: . . . but so next inning we figured you'd have to flip some guys too.

An umpires' conference.

PANNING the crowd: rowdy, vituperative booing.

The BOY booing too.

END OF FLASHBACK

ZAJAK's face, in the present. Confused.

BOY'S VOICE: . . . to, you know, to kind of retaliate.

ZAJAK (*Not really listening*): Right.

BOY'S VOICE: You remember?

ZAJAK's face. He's trying to, hard.

FLASHBACK. Comiskey Park. Day.

A White Sox homerun, left-centerfield upper deck.

Pandemonium.

The exploding scoreboard punctuates the roar of the crowd.

TERESA and JESSE, standing in their box to the left of the White Sox dugout, applauding and cheering with gusto.

ZAJAK's face, smiling. Congratulates teammate in dugout.

Blip blip.

The White Sox execute a 3–6–1 double play, eliciting a thunderous roar of approval.

A screaming line drive is caught by the shortstop at the top of his leap.

BOY'S VOICE: Had your at-em ball working that inning.

END OF FLASHBACK

ZAJAK blinks, in the present.

He looks at the BOY.

POV: The BOY is talking with great animation and excitement, but no sound comes out of his mouth.

FLASHBACK. Comiskey Park. Day.

The Hawk, in the booth, with Don Drysdale.

Nancy Faust at her organ.

Reds batter being hit by a pitch thrown by ZAJAK.

Then a series of very fast cuts: the Hancock Building. TERESA and JESSE. Room 321 of Wesley's intensive-care unit. The *Batcolumn*. The pair of rear admirals. The Water Tower. The face of the Guardian Angel. A Roger Brown skyline. A Chattering Man. TERESA. The face of the Guardian Angel.

BOY'S VOICE: . . . must've just winged him or something.

Reds trainer spraying hit batsman's biceps with Pro-Cain.

Blip blip.

Another Reds batter goes down. (We see this in negative image.)

The start of a fifty-man rhubarb.

END OF FLASHBACK

ZAJAK's face, in the present.

BOY'S VOICE: Remember?

FLASHBACK. Comiskey Park. Day.

A White Sox batter triples to deepest right-center: the play at third base is real close.

A major-league popup. The runner at third has to hold.

ZAJAK strides into the lefthanded batter's box. Crowd responds with standing ovation.

The third-base coach touches his heart with his left hand, his thigh with his right hand, crosses his arms, then touches the top of his cap.

BOY'S VOICE: Suicide squeeze time.

The third-base coach continues his sequence: tugs at his ear, touches the bill of his cap, strokes the SOX letters across the chest of his jersey. Then spits.

POV lefthanded batter's box: six-foot six-inch MASON MARIETTA leering down in at you, hard, from the top of the eighteen-inch mound. The scoreboard and stormclouds behind him. He seems right on top of you.

MARIETTA throws down the rosin bag.

The third-base coach has his back to you.

MARIETTA expectorates toward you.

Droplets of rain explode off your bat.

The runner at third increases his lead down the line.

BOY'S VOICE: First time you been up in a while.

MARIETTA's first pitch is an enormous jughandled curveball that forces you to turn back and duck—and then breaks down and over the plate.

The umpire roars out a strike call.

BOY'S VOICE: . . . starts you out with one of his hoo-doo balls.

The third-base coach goes through the same sequence of signs: the only difference is that this time he looks more insistent.

WHAT WE SEE FROM NOW ON WE WILL SEE IN A MOONY AND SILENT SLOW MOTION:

TERESA and JESSE. TERESA is in the process of blinking (the film is that slow), and JESSE has his fingers pressed down on his teeth and is whistling.

Three figure-8s with the barrel of the bat through the strike zone.

MARIETTA glares in for the sign, waits, shakes it off.

BOY'S VOICE: You must've been hoping there was gonna be, you know, DHs or something.

MARIETTA gets another sign, smiles, starts to nod vigorously.

MARIETTA checks the runner at third, then rocks into his motion.

BOY'S VOICE: Whole thing was hairy as heck.

MARIETTA begins his delivery.

THE FILM-SPEED SLOWS DOWN EVEN FURTHER AS THE PITCH STARTS TO COME:

The ball, up and inside to begin with, starts tailing up in toward your head.

MARIETTA grimaces, jerks, follows through.

The ball now appears to get larger.

The ball is still rising.

The ball is almost on top of you now.

The ball's an enormous white blur, eclipsing your view of all else.

BOY'S VOICE: ... and then BANG! (*There's also a thunderclap, lightning.*)

END OF FLASHBACK

143

ZAJAK's face, in the present. He blinks. No expression.

BOY'S VOICE (*While clapping his hands*): Down you go. . . . First you don't move at all, then you start twisting and shaking. . . . Whole place gets incredibly quiet.

ZAJAK (*Expressionless monotone*): What happened then.

BOY'S VOICE: Nothing, man. Nothing. . . . Place gets all quiet, rain's pouring down like a mother. They ended up carting you off on a stretcher. Looked like—

ZAJAK: Who won the game.

BOY'S VOICE: Looked like you might even've been, you know, *dead* or something.

ZAJAK: Who won the game.

Pause.

BOY'S VOICE: Game got rained out. . . . It rained all that day, rained all that night. Rained the next morning—

ZAJAK: And so—

BOY'S VOICE: So but that's when all this *other* junk started.

ZAJAK: So the game . . . just—

BOY'S VOICE: Just got rained out.

ZAJAK's face, impassive, unblinking.

The HARP PLAYERS' slow blues continues.

CUT TO:

Jesse and Maggie walk east on North Avenue past the cardinal's huge mansion, mostly in silence, toward Maggie's new stepfather's condo. Jesse's erection dismays him. I mean what's it doing? he wonders. He tries to walk normal. No way.

A chevron of mallards appears in the sky to their right, headed west. (A googolplex cubed, Jesse's thinking. Or, even worse, to the googolplexthed power. Just zillions and zillions and zillions.) He follows their flight for a while, focusing in on ∞, then happens to glance down downtown at the Hancock. (His dad is still down at that hospital, and the whole situation is starting to get to him now.) But what grabs his attention for the next fourth or third of a second is *this bright yellow speck* sort of drifting along down the Hancock. (His eyes are that good.) He follows its progress until, about two-fifths of its way down the Hancock, the roof of the cardinal's garage cuts it off. He forgets it. (His span of attention's that short.) He glances back up at the mallards, then down at the Hancock, then over at Maggie again. He hasn't refocused just yet, nor quite figured out what to say, but senses he'll come up with *something* if they just keep on walking and looking.

No way.

Teresa doesn't want Jesse to die.

She just doesn't want him to.

She does not want her Jesso to die.

Hunan, Kham Ping's young son, is knelt in the gravel before her. It is announced he is guilty of attending a school in the city. Using the legs of his great-great-grandmother's table, three Khmer Rouge soldiers start clubbing Hunan to the ground. Kham Ping is restrained by two others.

During the beating, Hunan's left eye somehow pops out. Noticing this, one of the soldiers calls for a halt to the blows and kneels by the body. She picks Hunan's eye from out of the gore, rolls it around on her palm, then deftly tosses it up to Kham Ping—who, in her daze, accidentally-on-purpose manages to catch it.

Inside her hand, what's left of the eye does not proceed to sprout wings and soar heavenward. It teaches no one in the city to see, for it cannot see itself. It does not reveal to Kham Ping any secrets. Nor does it disintegrate into a vapor, scalding the hand of its mother. It does not teach the soldiers a lesson.

For two days Kham Ping wanders the deserted streets of the city, clutching the eye of her son.

Maggie and Jesse are nervous. They've just turned the corner off North onto Astor when some whited-out public school kid lurches by them with Hendrix's ritual version of "The Star-Spangled Banner" wha-wha-whanging and bursting and toggling from a battered old Sanyo MX. It's the first and last time either Jesse or Maggie will hear it. But that's not the reason they're nervous.

And then all of a sudden it happens. They do it. They stop on the sidewalk in front of Maggie's new stepfather's building, fiddle with each other's fingers, and kiss. Killerdiller. Their tongues even touch for a second, but as soon as they do there's this really strange flavor that draws them against one another, makes them tilt sideways and back.

That was awesome, thinks Jesse, still holding onto her fingers. I mean, that was really incredible.

"I gotta go in now," goes Maggie, grinning a little. "Like I really do have to go in now."

Teresa can't help it. The churn in her brain has been flashing her back to a series of groaning and sweaty duets, complete with her and Raymondo's most private and personal code words and phrases and rules, to some things that she'd rather not dwell on right now but nonetheless can't quite phase out. It's perverse. Because the harder she struggles to keep certain episodes under, the quicker and fresher the mnemonic bytes effervesce.

For example. Either might balk at the outset, protesting they're GONNA BE LATE, since as often as not it begins as they're on their way out. Ray will be thoroughly naked, having just stepped from out of the shower, and into her own best silk panties will be all the further along she'll have got getting dressed. Somehow or other she'll wind up in front of him on their blue bedroom carpet in the midst of a strenuous set of her best FLEXIONES, making sure that her NIPPLES TOUCH CARPET each time, counting out loud to herself, pumping and straining and sweating. Raymondo JUST WATCHES. When she's done all she can, Raymondo goes to the second small drawer of her dresser and takes out two dice. One die is white, borrowed for keeps several years ago from Ray's uncle's Risk game. The other one's smaller, with more rounded corners, and red. (It was never real clear to her where this second die came from.) They call them

ZEE LOGS. Raymondo caresses and rotates them between his huge palms, shakes them around in his fist, looks at her, blows on them, then rolls them out onto the carpet. The number of FLEXIONES she's managed times the number of pips showing on top of ZEE LOGS becomes the MAGIC NUMBER Raymondo will have to perform in order to COME OUT ON TOP. Her average is seven or eight, although when she's desperate to win she has managed as many as twelve. But even if she only does seven, Raymondo, who averages forty-five to fifty, will still have to roll craps or less to keep within striking distance. (One time he'd rolled an eleven after she had done seven and made it all the way up to seventy-three and a half before collapsing. He'd had to pitch that night too.) Once he has started his set, she SUPERVISES every last one very closely, making darn sure those hard concave cheeks DON'T START RISING—if they do they get SNAPPED with his towel—that his chest TOUCHES DOWN every time. He usually is still going strong till around thirty-five, but it's right around then that he starts getting shaky, his rear end STARTS RISING, and so on. SNAP SNAP! By forty his biceps are trembling, his face is all red, and he's gasping. If he fails, as he so often does, to SATISFACTORILY PERFORM THE MAGIC NUMBER, she's got him. WITHOUT HAVING TO BE TOLD, his big chest still heaving, Raymondo rolls over and lies on his back for his TREATMENT, throughout which he stays wholly SERVILE TO HER COY DISDAIN. The first thing she does is she SMOTHERS him by straddling his still-gasping face, propelling herself back and forth over his nose and his mouth and his chin, eventually torquing down to the max in order to keep him from talking or moving or breathing. And meantime, of course, his own NEW DIRECTION is completely IGNORED AND NEGLECTED. The most she'll consent to is lightly and dispassionately running the side of her thumb up and down it, maybe stroking it with her wrist or her palm, BUT THAT'S ALL. And meantime she's riding his face like she's busting a bronco, but harder, till her teeth start to chatter in fact, at which point d'orgue she will jerk off her panties, slide right back up onto his HARDON, continue. If either could take it, this could go on forever, but of course neither can, so it doesn't. When at last she is through with him, Raymondo, UNREQUITED CAMSHAFT and all, is sent back to the shower to cool himself off and get dressed—or whatever. Her reason? THE RULES. And besides. They're ALREADY LATE AS IT IS.

If, on the other hand, Raymondo sur*passes* the MAGIC NUMBER (ties, of course, go to the woman), then it's *she* who's in trouble. BUT NO ROUGH STUFF, she'll say, half kidding, half pleading. No use. WITHOUT FURTHER ADO she'll be DOWN ON HER KNEECAPS and SHLURPING. Raymondo's behavior might include anything from straightforwardly PROVIDING DIRECTION, caressing her ears with his palms, to grabbing her hair, barking out orders and curses, to wielding the infamous NIPPLEWHIP. It goes without saying that throughout this ordeal her own POOR UNMENTIONABLE gets no stimulation whatever, oral or otherwise. None. She's compelled by THE RULES to

151

continue till she gets him to come, no matter how long he may take. They also provide that she KNOCK IT BACK GRATEFULLY, ALL OF IT, then lick off the series of AFTERSHOCKS. *Yum!*

For the most part these rules get adhered to. The one that gets broken most often, of course, is the one that provides that the loser be COOLLY NEGLECTED throughout the whole session. Her own biggest weakness is for sliding off Raymondo's cleft chin, shimmying down his sleek torso, then swinging around versy-arsy and giddying back up onto his ostensibly off-limits MOONBEAM, meanwhile, to make matters worse, greedily lapping his now comeslick features. DOMESTIC CRUDE city. It's so fun fun fun that 9.9 times out of ten she can't help it. Raymondo's most common transgression gets made in DIRECT RETALIATION, or so he will claim, for being INCISORED too hard, on the basis of which flimsy excuse he will gingerly remove MISTER MIKE from between her sharp choppers, shove her back down off her kneecaps, and pin her young ass to the carpet. Now she is *really* in trouble. For at this point he's got this quick, clever tackle-and-pulley maneuver whereby he forces her legs wide apart by scooping them up and then driving his body between them, shoving her thighs so far back in the process that her knees are on line with her shoulders, while at the same time he pinions her biceps beside her and hoists himself forward by pushing back down off her arms, yanking her torso in one direction while leaning down hard with his chest and his shoulders to double her back in the other. Wrenched open,

raised up, defenseless, she hopes that he won't be TOO
CRUEL. For Raymondo could sure go to town on her
now, give her one real hard time, simply by using the
same push-and-pull locomotion to jack up and stretch
out her gash as to drive his hard cock down and in,
tactically enhancing his thrust-to-weight ratio and at
the same time providing for strategically deep penetration. If she's lucky, that is. Because most of the time he
just holds her like this for a while, makes her wait, lets
that wet helpless feeling soak in. It's her SENTENCE.
She can protest all she wants about BREAKING THE
RULES, but they both know she's way overmatched
now: that the count's 0–2 and THE RULES have gone
right out the window: that once she is caught in these
hot ineluctable clutches he can tease her and zap her at
will. One of his wickedest tricks at this stage is to jam
her real slow for a bit, build up some rhythm, pretend
that he's finding his stroke, and then suddenly stop and
pull out. *O my God!* The soft pulsing void where his
hardon just was drives her nuts, but all she can do now
is tremble and writhe in short-circuit while he waggles
its tip on her stomach, bastes up her thighs with her
juices, and asks her HOW BAD DO YOU WANT IT. (She
knows that she best keep her throes to a minimum
now, but more often than not she just can't.) When
she gives him no answer he bites on her nipples, calls
her all sorts of lewd names, and jives her with more
false alarms: and she *still* won't admit that she wants it.
(She likes to make love with her husband, of course, in
mature, more conventional manners, but she likes it
much better when they fuck with each other, let

153

things get strange and depraved, so it's sinful and painful and raunchy: like they're not really married or something.) When he's darn good and ready he'll stick it back in, lean on her thighs even harder, and then drill her and warp her and rock her, make her quiver and gasp with some extra firm jolts high and tight. Make her ache. Make her shake. Make her come and cry out once or twice, quaking all out of control. Then maybe he'll let up a little, allow her to shiver and shudder, perhaps even put up a (doomed, futile, wonderful) struggle, while he pulls it back out one more time and starts slipping and sliding the whole throbbing length of it upside her clit, back and forth, flaunting his stalwart control, changing speeds, seering her, zinging her, first very slowly, so lightly, so deftly, now faster, now harder, now sideways—by now she is begging him, pleading—or dangles it just out of reach, making her arch up her back even more just to touch it. In the end he will fuck her, of course, long and hard—till she thinks she can't take any more, till she feels like she'll stay fucked forever—but in the frantic and desperate condition in which he's already got her she really can't wait that much longer. She has to, however. She can't, but she has to. She has to.

In any event, whoever has done the most pushups, whoever has broken THE RULES, or even if the dice weren't used in the first place, when they're through with each other Raymondo invariably LIES AND BREATHETH ON HER FACE, and God does she love that. She does.

They do not have a name for this game, but sometimes just the thought of it can burn in Teresa's warm blood like cold powdered glass, and she'll either have to get the game started or, if Ray's not around, just stand there and brace herself, like she's doing right now, rubbing her knuckles and blushing, doing her darnedest to blot out his moonbeam, his breathing, his stubbly slippery frictiony chin, and his face, staring out hard into space, till it passes.

Zajak pedals the twice-borrowed ten-speed steadfastly in second up Rush. Past gutted male strip joints, stalled cockeyed traffic, liquor stores still doing business. A small red-haired girl is pushing a black-hooded pram: she smiles up at Ray as he passes. People are clambering up and down fire escapes, across hoods of cars, engaged in some six-on-one fistfights. Zajak just wants to get home.

The Carnegie Theater's marquee announces a D. F. DeLay triple feature: *Wooden Shoes, China Lake,* and *The Lamberts* (of which Zajak has seen but the first). Just across Rush, on his right, is a thirteen-by-twenty-foot billboard featuring Gamma Ray Zajak himself—he is wearing his White Sox home jersey, raising his We're-Number-One finger, and is about to chomp down on a Wendy's bleu-cheese burger—but the real-life Ray Zajak rides by it without glancing up. Even if he were to, even without the amnesia, he probably wouldn't recognize the guy glancing back: aside from his ludicrous chomping expression, there's the fact that two of his teeth have been blackened, a crudely stitched Frankenstein scar is adorning one cheekbone, a bolt's sticking out of his neck, and the pitch of the daylight's producing a glare where his eyes are. He just shifts into third and pumps on.

A miniature peace march is just getting mobilized at the point at which Rush becomes State. Handpainted placards declaring END THE ARMS RACE/SAVE THE HUMAN RACE, MUSICIANS AGAINST NUCLEAR ARMS, PSR/NO MORE WAR, TIME TITHE, and GROUND ZERO are hoist, shaken, waved overhead. There are men sporting death masks, kids dressed as skeletons, women with fake melted faces. Unmasked persons are openly weeping. Others look grimly determined. The leaders, two women, are chanting at once into matching propane-powered megaphones, trying to get people started. Balking and sheepish at first, but soon with more confidence, the marchers begin to chant too:

> *One, two, three, four*
> *We don't want a nuclear war*
> *Five, six, seven, eight . . .*

but the next line's cacaphonous muddle: either *No need to retaliate* or *We want to negotiate*. Zajak can't tell. The two leaders lower their megaphones, glare at each other, and huddle. Gears clicking, handbraking, Zajak coasts past them, carefully zagging a course between marchers and watchers, wondering what might rhyme with twelve. Heading home.

In the alley between Zaxxon and Wag's a silver-haired gent in a Burberry macintosh suddenly pops up from under the galvanized lid of a trashcan and extends Zajak savage mal occhio. Zajak glares back for a second or two, but he's already thoroughly rattled. He tilts, drops his gaze, starts to wobble, and then almost tips over, but in the last split split second he's able to regain his balance. Ride on.

157

Teresa spots Jesse at the corner of Burton and State. He's just moping along, as per usual, intent on avoiding the cracks in the sidewalk or some such oblivious business, dangling his mitt from his pinkie.

Jesse spots *her* now. She's limping and puffing, with a dark ring of wetness on the chest of her sweatshirt against which her nipples are showing. Like always. Two smaller sweatrings are spreading out under her arms.

They go to each other.

"What's with your leg?"

A siren goes off up the block, then another: two more plucked notes on the zither of heard pandemonium, so that mother and son have to shout.

"So where were you?"

He shrugs. "So but what about Daddy?" His voice doesn't crack. "I mean, he's still down there and all."

"I know," shouts Teresa. She's hurting all over. She's hot. "I don't know."

They start heading home.

"You know that girl Maggie?" shouts Jesse.

STRICT TIME

JFK reappears. Just long enough for one speech. Very
short. There's something he wants to clear up. He
coughs up some blood, clears what is left of his throat.
"I am not, strictly speaking, a doughnut," he gargles.
And then, in a rose-colored shimmering flash, off he
fucks.

Ecstatic they're finally home, Teresa forgets for a moment about what's going on, about Ray. She fishes the keys from her pocket and unlocks the front door. They go in.

Blindsided now by an ashening vision, she imagines them buried alive. Gagged cries of odors rise up to her nose from her son as she stares at the wicked lead blue of his eyes.

Jesso's eyes are his father's. His father's.

She wants to know who'll close his father's.

At last. The 1300 block of North State. After passing the Ambassador East, on his right, and the Ambassador West, on his left, Zajak rides by a series of graystones and redstones and brownstones, all very fancy and gracious. He lives around here? Well well well. He zeroes in hard on addresses, excited, closing in fast on his own.

The street, on his left, is a great disorder: taxis and limos parked stalled and crashed every which way, cars spilling over the curb, freshly whacked citizens draped over hoods and out doors: crude tableaux. He maneuvers the bike up the sidewalk, carefully steering past half-naked rollerboys, panicked old geezers, and toddlers. His neighbors, he guesses. One little girl, all alone, is crying so hard she cannot catch her breath. Zajak swerves past her, cursing the mother for abandoning such a helpless young child, and rides on.

He can just see the lake, on his right, as he gets off and walks across Banks. A Volvo with bodies still in it's on fire. Zajak can smell burning gas, burning hair, though he can't hardly look as the charred-off black stumps of the arms of the driver get warped and consumed by the heat. He climbs back up on the bike, takes one last short look at the lake, and rides on.

A yumpy-looking couple in compleat jogging gear—headphones, bright yellow sweatbands, matching green Gore-Tex ensembles—appear on their porch at the corner of Banks and North State. Zajak notes their address—1351! almost there—then happens to notice that their blinds are all drawn, inferring (correctly) that the dummies must still be oblivious to what's going down. For they're already jogging in place, adjusting the volume controls on their headphones, when the scene on the street finally hits them.

And Zajak, pumped up now, rides on.

Jesse goes into the kitchen—having first ascertained that his mother's not in there—and starts pulling out drawers and going through cabinets for matches.

A late summer fly buzzes past him, circles his head, nicks his ear. He slaps at it, dodging and cursing, thinking it might be a wasp. When he sees that it's not he ignores it, or tries to, and steps up his search for the matches.

The fly finally lands on the counter, about a foot and a half from his hand. He stares at it, galvanized, as it frics its front legs back and forth, its dark bright green back reflecting the light from the window. It's weird. He's convinced for some reason that it's preparing to shit on the counter. (It's not. What it is is an envoy* with news of his dad, of his Maggie.) Slowly, real slowly, he moves his hand closer. He's pissed.

His hand flashes open and, the next thing he knows, the fly's buzzing inside his fist. He's amazed that he caught it, at the way that it vibrates and tickles. He shakes it up next to his ear, making sure, then hurls it down onto the floor. He feels pretty proud of himself.

The fly's still alive, but it's stunned. It can't talk. It

163

*envoy extraordinary and minister plenipotentiary

staggers around in a circle, tries to take off once or twice. Doesn't work.

Jesse squats down, watching it try to recover, then gets down on his hands and his knees and looks closer.

And it finally dawns on him now what he's done.

Since INCRBIMs take longer to reach certain cities, it's only just now, right this instant, that one Helen Swissmiss, Zajak's main squeeze in KC, unalloyed Royals fan, twenty, KCAI sculpture major, girl with the amazingly funzy and delicate modulations in her voice, the flawless and translucent skin, who always had the Baby Ruth bar and the freshly squeezed GJ for breakfast, made the strange little sculptures of dogs, one with the ultrasensitive backs of her knees, wore her bangs in her eyes all the time, has been wasted: tanned, crisped, blinded, hydrogenated, and vaporized all in about a third of a second whilst reading da Vinci and thinking of Zajak and biting into an unripe fall nectarine with her slim tan bare ankles swinging crossed and submerged back and forth in the Warwick Fountain's clear shallow pool. Like that. The fountain itself turns to magma. Like that. The pool turns to steam, an ultrafine mist, rising up into the light. Just like that.

1367.

Zajak dismounts, puts down the cold metal kickstand, and shivers. He's begun to feel more and more woozy, but he thinks nothing of it. He's made it. He retrieves the directory page from his bloomers, rechecks the address, then squints at the door's pewter numerals. As soon as he gets them in focus, he sees that it all matches up.

The house is gray stone, three stories high, with black trim. Two little gables up top. Six of the windows have white lacy curtains, the two first-floor large ones have blinds. He hopes against hope that it's home.

On the sidewalk to his left, by the corner, are four little girls playing hopscotch, hopping and bobbing and counting with a deadly seriousness that makes Zajak almost, well, laugh. Are they kids of his neighbors? They must be.

"How you ladies doing this morning?"

The two smallest ones both ignore him. The third glances up at his outfit, confused. The fourth stares right at him and smiles.

"O hi, Mr. Zajak."

One of the little ones mumbles down into her chest: something like *lowmizajax*. The other one giggles.

"Home from school early this morning?"

Dead silence.

"How's the game going?"

"Fine."

"Okay."

"Fine."

Zajak now feels very dizzy. *At hopscotch the trees are the bells of a plumb line which at each meal a tune on the violin carries off at each stop, and spins a web of violins sewn to the lilac fringe of a widespread group of hunters, of cobalt rocks and necklaces of sea urchins attached to each leaf overflowing on the stretch of wall near the clock, and the incompatible wounds and the whiplash*

"So, who's winning?"

"Jeannette is."

"Wendy is."

"I am."

Salted anchovies of the wide road of memories, chopped small on the marble covered with graffiti from so many dawns, abandoned at the end of a row of cups full of blind

"Say, any of you happen to see *Mrs.* Zajak this morning?"

Two little nods.

He shivers again, shakes away some of his faintness.

"Yup, just came home."

"No, she is up on the roof of the house."

He looks. No one there. Feels naïve.

"I think I just saw her with Jesse with her just a coupla minutes ago."

Jessie. He's sweating. Who's Jessie.

"With Jessie?"

167

"Mm hmm."

So. What. A wife. But does that mean. That with her. A daughter?

"Were they, do you remember if they were, ahm, going out or, or you know, or coming back in?"

"In."

Or a lover.

"Yeah in, I think."

"In."

Or a husband.

"Thanks," he says, glancing back up at the roof. "Thanks a lot."

"Sure."

"Welcome."

Or.

"How's your head?"

"Hey . . ."

A son.

Still in the kitchen, Jesse plows through the junk drawer for matches. There are none. What he pulls out instead is the yellowing Mother's Day card he'd made in third grade for Teresa. He unfolds it and reads it:

MOTHER

M   mondo   musician   magnificent
O   out of this world   outragess   outstanding
T   thoughtfull   tremendess   terrific
H   helpfull   happy   harmless
E   excellent   enchanting   entertaining
R   respectfull   relistic   remarkable

Love,
Jesse

He folds it back up and stuffs it down into his pocket, then continues to riffle the trilevel chaos for matches.

Zajak knocks once on the stained oaken door while he looks up and down for the buzzer. Can't find it. His head is now (literally) killing him. He knocks two more times, almost gives up, and then spots it. It's right where it should be, of course, facing out from the jamb plain as day at a point right in line with his elbow. He mentally palms himself in the forehead as it starts to sink in just how zonked he must be not to've noticed it earlier, then imagines the jolt he'd've felt if he'd actually palmed himself there. He exhales and inhales, summons what presence of mind he has left, then pushes the buzzer three times.

Fifteen seconds go by. No one answers.

And but then there's a noise, then a voice, then a creak of a foot on a floorboard or stair. Information.

He knocks five more times, *dot da da dah dah,* leaving the familiar tattoo unresolved. He's excited.

He hears a chain rattle and a big deadbolt lock get released. There are voices. He's pushing his hair off his forehead, wondering six things at once, and contracting his abdominal muscles when the door gets pulled open and he finds himself facing a boy and, just behind him, a woman. The boy's face is bony, with grayish blue eyes. Pretty tall. The woman he really can't see yet.

The boy steps aside, blurting out something that

Zajak can't catch. He focuses in on the woman, taking her face in. Her eyes.

"How on earth," she starts saying. It's clear she is shocked. "Come in. Just come in."

He balks for a couple of seconds, hitches up the waist of his bloomers, goes in.

The boy shuts the door. "What's with the T-shirt?" he says.

But Zajak can't answer. Behind the boy's shoulder there's a strange little shelf sticking out from the wall of the foyer on which a foot-high Dalmatian is sitting with one front paw raised and extended. It seems to be staring right at him—and begging. What he finds even stranger is that both shelf and Dalmatian are painted with the same spotted black-on-white pattern.

"Hey," says the woman, to Zajak. She touches his famous cleft chin. "You okay?"

He blinks, smiles, and nods, trying to think what to say.

She puts her hands onto his waist and starts to embrace him, but he doesn't know how to react. It's her face. He thinks it's pure gorgeous, the best face he's ever laid eyes on, and he wants to believe it's his wife's. And to hold her. To have her. But his uncertain jitters and stiffness abort her attempt at the hug. He can't help it.

"Mondo?" she says.

They just stare at each other.

Then, without pressure or moisture, they kiss.

"I was in a hospital," he says, pulling back. He

wants to explain what has happened. "But so, I came home."

"You . . . came home," says the woman.

"How'd you get here," the boy wants to know. Shakes his head. "I mean, jeez."

Zajak can't say. He feels his heart blipping and seizing. He's white.

"So you know me," he says.

The boy and the woman just look at each other, and but all of a sudden, to Zajak, they appear sort of greenish and way way way way out of focus.

"We *know* you?"

He starts to pass out. His mouth works to warn them, to ask for some help, but not much but moaning comes out. As his body torques sideways he tries to sit down, to break his collapse with his palms.

Doesn't work.

NOW MORE THAN EVER

All that short fall no
Just could not talk normal
All that short fall yeah
Was burning to be gone

Na na na na
Na na na na
Hey hey hey
Good bye

Bloodshot blind azures
His dose of cyan-ide
The Saybrook Kid herself
Been taken for a ride

Na na na na
Na na na na
Hey hey hey
Good bye

Greathearted Eurymedon's great-great-great-
    granddaughter
Has now got this smoldering love jones
For the thoughtful young son of Penelope
Who'd like to no dra ha her scones

Na na na na
Na na na na
Hey hey hey
Good bye

But now the day is over
And something's drawing nigh
The something something somethings
Steal across the sky

Na na na na
Na na na na
Hey hey hey
Good bye

Na na na na
Na na na na
Hey hey hey
Good bye

They lug him and drag him and carry him into the familyroom, where it's carpeted, then lie him down facing straight up. He's breathing but no longer moaning. They're scared.

Drip drip drip.

It occurs to Teresa that the head of his bed down at Wesley had been raised about thirty degrees, so she props up his neck with a pillow. But now what? About every half hour or so a nurse had come in and done things like pull back his eyelids to measure his pupils' dilation, or taken his pulse or his blood pressure, or tweaked one or both of his nipples. Teresa tries tweaking the left one, but since she really doesn't know what to look for, she stops and starts stroking his chest. Then his forehead. She's sweating. One nurse had checked for something she called the Babinski reflex by taking a stiff piece of cardboard and scraping the soles of his feet: if the toes on his left foot flared out, it meant there was irritation on the right side of his brain, and vice versa. Or something like that. She wishes she'd paid more attention to what the nurses and doctors were saying and doing instead of just sitting there watching Ray's face, or staring at the graph lines and blips on the monitors, or praying for him to come to. Because now that he has and come home, she's got no idea what she should do.

By now Ray is shaking all over. Drool's foaming up

175

from between his clenched teeth, his eyes are rolled back in his head, there's blood oozing out his right ear.

Jesse can't take it. "Shit, make it stop!" he insists. "Close his eyes!"

"Okay, okay. There." And she does it. It gives her the willies. She's crying. "Calm down!"

"Jesus," says Jesse. He stands up and shivers. He's white. It looks like he might start to vomit.

He does.

WHAT THE HOLY GHOST HAS TRANSMITTED

The atmospherics have to be just about perfect to be able to hear the HG, for he communicates with us via the shortest of all the Gespensterwellen. So close your eyes tight, prick up your soul, and tune in. His white mojo wings tuck themselves back, his tantalum beak starts to vibrate, and out zips his wisdom in quick bits of digital info. He informs us, for example, that the phenoms are no longer phenomenating, that the melanzans, for once, ain't responsible. He tells us as well that a bright fire shall arise from small beginnings and shall rapidly become great and with its terrific silence shall stun all those within earshot and with its breath it shall blind lovely womans and hydrogenate their cities and fountains. He concludes this particular memo by reminding us that Lucifer took his music with him from Paradise, but that even in Hell, as Bosch showed, it was able to represent Paradise and become bride of the cosmos. Amen.

Teresa remembers that on the day she'd met Ray her elbows and knuckles were killing her. Even back then. It was a Tuesday, May 9, about 10:45 in the morning. His father was tuning Namgae's (her roommate's) piano and Ray'd come along for the company. For the first half an hour or so she hadn't even known he was there. She'd stayed down the hall in her bedroom, rehearsing her end of the allegrissimo movement of Prokofiev's *Back in the USSR* sonata, then had literally bumped into him as they were both on their way to the kitchen.

Ray was wearing a navy blue suit, a dark green silk tie, a pinpoint cotton blue shirt. (He'd just been on television.) He was tall. It looked like he'd just got a haircut.

In the kitchen he told her his name, what he was doing there, asked if he might use the phone. His voice sounded nervous. His eyes were slate blue. She said yes.

She remembers all this very clearly, too clearly, as Ray now lays dying.

She remembers what she had on too: no socks or shoes, cut-off white Levi's, a navy blue NYU sweatshirt. She had not washed her hair yet that morning, and for this she was silently cursing herself.

She never had heard of Ray Zajak, but while her tea

water boiled she eavesdropped right in on his call. The person on the other end of the line, some guy named Roberto, was the one doing most of the talking, so there wasn't a lot to find out. She remembers how much it relieved her that the person he'd called wasn't female.

Namgae then came into the kitchen and you could tell that she'd put on mascara. Ray said so long to Roberto and hung up the phone. He thanked Namgae, thanked Teresa, for letting him use it, then headed back out to the livingroom.

The kettle now started to whistle.

"Hey, want some tea?" called Teresa.

"Pluck me whilst I blush," Namgae whispered. In the three years Teresa had known her, it was the first time Namgae had spoken or behaved in a way even remotely suggestive of lust. And besides. She already had Dr. Hudson.

"Not really," said Ray. "Hey. But thanks," then headed again down the hallway.

Hey. But thanks.

Namgae and Teresa just looked at each other.

"O boy."

Fourteen months later their Jesso'd been born. She remembers. How big he had felt but how small he had turned out to be.

She remembers that on the day she met Ray her old Lamee bow had just been rehaired with good Russian. She remembers having carefully wiped the used rosin from the strings and the fingerboard of the fiddle her father had bought her with the money from some weird insurance policy after her mother had died. Her Vuillaume.

She also remembers her absolute certainty that Namgae's tuner's tall son would soon call, that in spite of her absolute pitch and long years of practice and study her arthritis would end her career before it could really begin, and that these things would happen to *her*. She can actually picture herself *blip blip blip* and so meantime, slumped in a whirlpool that same afternoon in the Comiskey Park visitors training room, the Ray she remembers was thoughtfully peeling and sectioning a thick-skinned pink grapefruit, a gift from some fan. He could picture Namgae. The Blue Jays were playing the White Sox that evening on local TV, but Ray was not pitching. He could picture Teresa. He put down the grapefruit, picked up his hard little black rubber ball, and started methodically squeezing. He did not like grapefruit. He wanted to pitch, and Teresa. On the other hand, Namgae wasn't all that bad either.

But the thing that concerned him the most was his season: his stats, his career, his whole future. Two weeks before, while making only his third start of the season, he'd badly torn a groin muscle while fielding a bunt on the slick artificial turf in Seattle and landed himself on the twenty-one-day disabled list. Five or six starts down the tubes, just like that. It was his first real injury since his football days back in high school, and he wasn't real pleased. He'd continued traveling with the team, however: suiting up, playing pepper, charting pitches and scouting the other teams' hitters, trying to make himself useful for the incredible salary the Blue Jays were already paying him. And his teammates were winning: 9–4 since he'd left the rotation, 13–6 overall, with ten of those wins on the road. What killed him was not knowing what might not happen, or happen, to *him.*

It was only his second full season. He'd been 18–8 as a rookie, with a 2.64 ERA, 7.85 MBA, and 239 strikeouts. The sabermetricians went crazy. He'd also pitched four one-hitters, a record, of which he'd only won two, which was also a record. American League Rookie of the Year by a landslide. Two *Sports Illustrated* covers: one solo, the second with three other Blue Jays. Missed the Cy Young Award by six votes.

What he wanted most desperately now was to keep all this up, to recover and still have his stuff. There was no real good reason, of course, to assume that he wouldn't, but still. He tried not to think about that, to wonder instead about calling Namgae or Teresa. He'd taken their number from his father's little green clients' address book, but he didn't know which one would answer.

He got out of the whirlpool, covered himself with a towel, and was snapped by two more as he walked to his locker. He yanked off his own and snapped back. A red plastic floor-hockey puck hit his shin and ricocheted into his locker. He retrieved it and fired it back at the shooter. A *Sun-Times* reporter wanted to know how his groin was. He turned round and belched. Then he sat down and plunged his left fist, wrist, and forearm into his portable barrel of rice, clenching and twisting and driving with all of his frustrated might. He was thinking.

He'd already been given two nicknames: The Canada Arm (which he lost four years later when his agent finally got him into a pitcher's park and he signed with the White Sox for what came to just under his weight in pure gold the first year, then went up) and Gamma Ray Zajak. The second one stuck. The ray in question referred to his high riding hummer that brought the white ball from the cross-seamed release point of his hard-to-read three-quarter lefthanded buggywhip delivery to the heart of the heart of the strike zone—although sometimes above and inside it—at (according to Ted Turner's SzorcGun at least) 98.89 miles an hour. In about a third of a second, in other words, about the time it took hitters to blink.

Or to duck. Because that was the thing about Ray, even then. In addition to having decent control of his foshball and screwgie, he was also real wicked and sudden. Or, as Don Drysdale had rhetorically wondered that Tuesday on Channel 32 while reviewing the Blue Jays' rotation: "Does young Mr. Zajak have a control problem or's he just flat *mean*?" Drysdale then chuckled and snorted as the station had segued to Warner Wolf's comic slow-motion montage of Zajak upending a half-dozen batters. For the fact of the matter was that in 234.2 innings the previous season Ray had walked only forty-nine batters, twenty intentionally, but had *hit* thirty-six. "Ray'll come at you," his manager, Roberto Raritan, had admitted the previous evening to Howard Cosell on *Monday Night Baseball.* "There's no doubt about it. But tactical jamming systems are strictly preemptive, ad hoc, and since velocity and location are the matrix mechanics of pitching, there's always that trace of uncertainty." Cosell'd said, "Say what?" and then cackled. Ray's own rationale for the media—when they forced him to give one—was that, while he never had thrown at a hitter on purpose, if he saw a guy really dig in he would naturally start to get nervous and was thus prone to lose some control. Jays catcher Vin Da Capo had put it less coyly for a *Sporting News* feature on Ray: "Sucker comes up tries to sit on Ray's smoke we fug him and play him some chin music." Drysdale, himself a notorious headhunter back in his playing days with the Dodgers, had summed it up thusly to an amused Kenny Harrelson as the montage of knockdowns concluded: "Listen, it's always been part of the game, Hawk. You know that." Harrelson whewed and agreed. "Yessir," he drawled. "That ol fear of music. Though you *know* the kid pulled this kind of stuff over in the National League, where he'd have to stand in and hit for himself, he'd last about what? Three or four innings at most."

Teresa, of course, was watching this broadcast with interest, even though she'd never been much of a sports fan till Namgae'd tipped her off about Ray after he and his father had left. There she was, nonetheless, crouched on the edge of the sofa, munching unsalted cashews, alone—Namgae had just lost a coin flip and been forced to dash the half block to Gim Bop's and pick up their be bim bop orders—doing her darnedest

183

to make what these two hick announcers were saying make sense, when lo and behold the young Mr. Zajak himself called her up, just as she'd known that he would. (The Gespensterwellen she always stayed keyed to had never been stronger or clearer.) Ray had been able to sneak from the dugout in the top of the second and was using the payphone outside the visitors locker room. It was eight after eight, almost exactly nine hours since they'd seen one another, and Teresa's nervous and calm systems were suddenly both in an uproar. As were, of course, Ray's, only worse. But Teresa remembers that before he could even get started with his hemming and hawing she came straight out and asked him what chin music was. And, hawing and hemming, he told her.

Blip blip.

Teresa and Ray are on much the same wavelength apparently, because this same conversation has begun to come back to Ray too, but with one big big difference: while Teresa can picture their whole long first Tuesday together in detail, all Ray can recall through the damp gauzy veil of his fugue state are the distinctly unvisual contours of some nervewracking phonecall, then nothing, as the stuporous neurons in his pineal gland and his pons mince ritardando on laser-sharp edges of coma. *Drip drip.* A slightly less floppy mnemonics, however, would go on to reveal that the nervewracking phonecall led directly to dinner that very same night up at Grunts, as s/he segues again (flashing back day for night through undulating midnight blue filter) to:

184

Their virtually simultaneous arrival in two separate taxis at the corner of Park West and Dickens. Raymondo was rocking a new tight black knit Izod shirt and almost-new Levi's. No belt. His definition and muscle tone were simply astonishing, but he still didn't look unintelligent. Teresa was fetching in Namgae's clingy light black Gore-Tex skirt, very short, and a plain white men's cotton T-shirt. Perfume by Issey Miyake. Their hair was still wet. With put-on sangfroid they proclaimed they were starving, went in. Two people recognized Ray, but he suavely declined to sign autographs.

They were given a booth in the corner. Ray ordered sole, Teresa the mushroom bleu-cheese burger. The busboy poured water. Teresa looked under the ashtray and discovered a CTA transfer. She folded it, played with it, saved it (still has it, in fact, in some drawer). They smiled at each other. Preliminary dialogue continued to be awkward and tentative (they mocked the decor, for example, proclaimed once again they were starving), but as they were standing in line for the salad bar they somehow got on to Ray's father, the half-blind old tuner who'd got them together. And that broke the ice. Teresa was touched by the fact that when the Blue Jays played games in Chicago Ray always stayed in the condo he'd bought for his dad on Pine Grove: smack in the center of Buttland, she noted. Ray's dad was fifty, Teresa's just seven months younger. Both of their mothers were dead, it turned out: both of cancer. Neither had brothers or sisters but always had wanted to have them. Okay. They relaxed.

Subsequent conversation touched on Anderson, Carter, the Blue Jays, the service, the salad, the president's three cardiologists, Namgae Kim, Dr. Hudson, inexpensive imitation 1952 Fender Telecasters, beta shades, urban sax, bottom, Richard Nixon, stiff plastic discs, and the blues, but eventually and inevitably on "putting a little hair on the ball" and "showing a guy Bobby Brown," which Ray "sort of" supposed were the "principal canon" of his "private religion." Teresa was charmed but dismayed. She found this "too strange." Ray tried to drop it, but she just wouldn't let him. (She was really impressed by this big hunk's vocabulary in discussing such violent behavior.) She ironically begged to hear more about "clunking guys" upside the head "for no earthly reason at all." By now Ray was much too embarrassed. He started to detail instead the subtle advantages of being lefthanded in baseball and racquet sports, but Teresa would not be put off. She mentioned the cello, confounding him further, then told him pointblank he was "cruel"—she'd meant to say "mean," quoting Drysdale. "And what's this about fear of music?" What could Ray say? Eye contact and body language were held to a minimum for the next several minutes. Ray tried to wax euphemistic: the result was a series of silences each more discrete than the last one. They tried to talk music again, but Ray's jockish tastes were revealed to be too unso-

phisticated. Neither Teresa's barely clothed singularities or Ray's bulging and naked left forearm ever came up. Nor did the latter's groiner or the former's arthritis. It was starting to get pretty tense. The ice was once again broken, however, when the latest bad Jesus joke was expertly sprung by Teresa (apropos of Ray's frank admission that "Jeez, am I nervous," she bigly admitted that she too was nervous then gnawed on the back of her palm and asked him, "Who's this?" Ray was too rattled to guess. Teresa kept gnawing: "I mean, speaking of *nervous,* who's this?" But Ray had no clue. "Jesus biting his nails," said Teresa) and which Ray, at first, didn't get, but then found so awful he gagged on his sole, snorting out some through his nose. The food was okay. The service was fine. Neither one smoked after dinner because neither of them was on fire. (That one was Ray's.) Lime-flavored bombes topped with chocolate were ordered by both for dessert, but just picked at. Check paid by Ray, tip by Teresa. No drinks.

Back at Teresa's apartment (which Namgae had graciously vacated) they listened sedately to Priaulx Rainier's "Quanta" and, less sedately, to Nile Mansions' cover of "Talk Talk," but somehow wound up tilted elbow to elbow over Namgae's old Baldwin for what was apparently, for Teresa at least, some dead serious, unsedate arm wrestling. Ray was victorious in four out of seven (righthanded) and Teresa was thereby compelled, according to ground rules laid down beforehand, to drop down posthaste on the carpet and give him six bona fide flexiones, exposing to Ray in the process a scratch on her thigh and the backs of her scrumpdiddleyumptious pink knees. Two awkward moments now followed, but Ray in the end got his chance to examine all the little doodads and things in Teresa's strange bathroom. It was Teresa's turn next, and she gargled. Later, strained groin and all, Ray was shamed, barely, by a gadulka-wielding Teresa into a macho jock's version of a truncated Slovakian czardas, leaving Teresa with no choice at all but to notice his sturdily independent rearend suspension system and how it just might allow for some extraordinary performance and handling. In a word, their respective excitements were mounting.

They kissed for the very first time at 2:22. They were still in the livingroom, dancing to no song at all, jammed up against one another. By 2:26 they were more or less prone on Teresa's made bed. *Blip blip blip.* 'Twas either on or within the not all that commodious vicinity of said maid's made bed that the certain lengths to which neither Ms. T nor Sir Mondo were prepared to go in order to facilitate innovative sexual intercourse between consenting adults remained unascertained, thus giving lie to the rumors that classical musicians of the female persuasion were frigid and that Polish men made terrible lovers because they insisted on waiting until the swelling went down. Love then took over and launched them on slippery particles of ecstasy into waves of celestial light, and they realized that nothing mattered at all except that as woman and man they were one, for now and throughout all eternity.

Yeah.

Jesse announces he's booking.

"Just got to," he says, at the door.

"Where to?" says Teresa. "And why?"

"Maggie's," says Jesse. His breath reeks of vomit and Scope. "I just got to."

"Now listen," she says, though by this point there's really not much that can phase her. "Wouldn't it really be better—"

They hug.

"Let's be careful out there."

"I'll be back."

She knows that he won't, but she nods, says okay. She even begins to let go.

MAGIC NUMBERS

Torches stand like spears on the skyline
So remember the wrath in the whirlwind.
Eta Carinae is all but invisible
Through the translucent haze over Texas.
And but then there was light.

Regular Hot Dots have already melted
On Gibsons in basements and studios
All over the Bronx. It's unreal.
Cincinnati's intact. So's Chicago,
St. Paul, Minneapolis.

But Anaheim Stadium is the only
Large building still standing in Anaheim.
And now there goes Seattle.
Like a shot off a shovel
A churchbell gets sounded in Oakland,

Just once.
Light rushes into the homes there
So the dead now are killing the living
Who remember the wrath in the whirlwind.
O boy.

Teresa is doing her darnedest not to break down. Not to talk to herself. To talk to herself, but just not out loud. To figure out what she should do.

She stands into spiraling vertigo. Her son has abandoned his parents, she really can't fathom what for. To smoke? To make out? To be able to die on his own? She does not have much will left to wonder. Her unconscious husband's laid out on the carpet, a ludicrous orange-clad sculpture thrown into high relief by available light and her headache, his familiar proportions now angled obliquely below her, skewed by her weird point of view. She can't stand to look any more.

When something is bothering her, under normal conditions at least, there are measures she brings into play more or less automatically to help make her feel better. The first thing she does is imagine herself as vividly and concretely as possible at the moment that will signal once and for all the end of what's bothering her, the point at which the unpleasure of the present will be officially past. What this does is gives her an actual time-and-space episode to start looking forward to. Next she promises herself to remember having looked forward to it once it has finally occurred. To help guarantee she'll remember, however, she first must come up with a mnemonic nexus, an associative cue she can count on to jog her memory of the original promise at the point of the unpleasure's passage.

The way that she helps herself cope with her bouts of premenstrual syndrome is as good an example as any of how all this works. The four or five days before she gets her period are not her best time of the month. Her forehead breaks out, her left breast gets tender, and her thighs and her guts and her joints and her throat all feel so swollen and oinkly that sometimes she can't hardly stand it. It's sickening. What's worse is the accompanying churn in her brain that makes her feel eminently capable of furious barehanded manslaughter over even the most trivial incident: fans calling Ray, flies in the house, Jesse's dumb haircuts. In other words, nothing. The mnemonic nexus thus becomes the enormous relief she knows she will feel when the thick backed-up blood finally starts soaking down out through her uterus. The relief she will feel in the future she uses to neutralize, or pay back, or cancel—or *something*—the discomfort she feels in the present. In the meantime, of course, she still has the physical symptoms, but she's much better off psychologically if she's able to zero in hard on their absence. Because the harder she concentrates now, the better she's able to savor the counterpoint between how clogged-up and buggy she feels at the moment and the glorious mollification she knows she will feel when the blood comes.

Similarly, during Ray's West Coast road trips the nexus is meeting his plane at O'Hare. Or, when her arthritis starts to get out of hand, it's Dr. Czyzinski's white-on-white waiting room and the subsequent bliss of the cortisone.

The measures are based on her theory that it does you no good at all in the long run for unpleasure to merely have passed if its passing goes unnoticed and, as a result, uncelebrated. She does not have a name for these measures, but she tends to think of them as a practical attempt to make virtues of certain adversities: pure antecedent and consequent, only worked in reverse. They admittedly fail to make premenstrual syndrome or rheumatoid arthritis attacks any less irritating, they don't even make them go away any faster, but they do make them slightly less hard to put up with.

For the last thirty seconds Teresa's been doing her best to deploy these same measures in response to her current unpleasure. The problem, of course, is that the only way they might be effective is if she can somehow convince herself in good faith that there's even the remotest of chances that she, Ray, and Jesso will not have to die—that everyone won't have to, really—and that things just might go back to normal. And but so far she hasn't been able to.

"What I find most astonishing," she says, to herself. Then she stops, breathes in deeply, and exhales.

She holds out both palms, turns them over, then closes her eyes and just freezes (again) as her billions and trillions of braincells begin to light out for the territories.

Seventeen seconds go by.

One of Ray's face muscles twitches. That's all.

Twenty seconds.

Eyes back wide open, still pretty shaky, Teresa

squats down by the bookshelves and thumbs through the racks of cassettes.

Let there be fiddles, she thinks.

Ray's current level of consciousness is comatose. Impossible to arouse by verbal stimulation or kisses. Flexing and localizing movements (MOEX2): none at all. Response to tactile stimulation such as tweaking or twisting of nipples: none at all. Internal audio portion: what sounds like a zither with seven silk strings being plucked through a phaser, glissando. Positive Babinski response on right sole. Best verbal reponse: none at all. Pupils fixed and dilated to 8.5 millimeters. Luminosity of internal visuals: pitch. Posterior tibial pulse: 110/20. Ventricular tachycardia tending toward cardiac standstill.

When Teresa inserts the cassette she's selected into Ray's new Nakamichi Dragon ZX (complete with six wolfram-trioxide heads, Z-Zero phase error, automatic azimuth correction, DD Double Dolby, and user-friendly zigzag control panel) she discovers there's no more electricity. So what else is new, she can't help but wonder, as she lurches and hobbles upstairs to find Jesse's crummy (but battery-powered) old Vox Box.

What's on this cassette, unless she's mistaken, is a hybrid version of Beethoven's Fugue in B-minor with the voice of the first violin left purposefully missing. Teresa had taped it back when she was still at the Conservatory off the copy of a friend of Namgae's who had gone to the Juilliard and whose professors had recorded it to provide their more advanced students with a challenging sequence of pitches to practice against. Or something like that: Teresa no longer remembers. A kind of makeshift bootleg play-along-with-the-Juilliard, then. Not the actual Robert Mann Juilliard, of course, with that dashing Joel Grossman on cello. But still.

She's excited.

Trish turns to vodka when Meryl tells Kevin she needs some more time to consider Matt's marriage proposal. At the club, Lucia and Judson's sexual attraction is obvious. Helen tells Ray she is pregnant and was married to Carlton. Palmer cuts himself shaving. Zeke informs Amy and Matt they've inherited Brunhilda's shares in Nero's TV station. Stunned, Palmer tells Trish that he wants a divorce. The Mossad decapitates Kevin, tosses his head from a helicopter, pins it on Judson and Matt, and offers to Meryl a whole new identity in exchange for her silence. With Nero's help, Zeke finds out just how difficult it is to really quit smoking. Matt, now in prison, has margarine forced up his nose when he tries to skull Judson. Lucia is questioned by Carlton about Palmer's new haircut.

Zajak comes to. It's a miracle. He even remembers his father, albeit briefly. The merest of glimmers of features, then nothing. He does not remember his son.

He looks at his wife, who is kneeling beside him, inserting a tape in a deck. In a hot flash of pain and nostalgia he remembers the contours of a similar episode, but without too much verisimilitude. And then, again, nothing.

Opening riffs, minus the first violin, *Grosse Fuge,* volume dial turned down to three. There were fiddles.

He rubs his right eye with the butt of his palm, hears the bloodshot conjunctiva toggle and creak with the cello, the dripping behind it continue. He's dying and knows it.

The exposition of the subject is driven ahead energetically, and he hears the three voices. He hears them and knows them. He senses that one voice is missing.

He notices floaters in his vitreous humor as he focuses in on his wife. He wonders if the static and hum in his head's from the tape. It is not.

The *Fuge* now hits fever pitch. Never mind.

He stares at Teresa's strange hair. At her eyes. At the line of her cheekbone. At the disarmingly wonderful gist of her breast through her shirt.

Nevermore.

The blue damask curtains are drawn, so it's dark in the familyroom now, more or less. But it's noon. And Jesse and Ray are both gone. Eyes open, scared, Teresa is listening hard to the tripled attack of the fiddles, getting set to stay dead a long time.

She turns up the Vox Box to nine, touches Ray's forehead, rests her bare neck on his shoulder. She just hopes it's quick. She is ready. She can tell from the Gespensterwellen that it's going to come any second.

Okay. Her gnarled, knobby fingers stir at her sides, fretting and bowing saltando along with the dismembered fugue. Any time.

Jesus, she thinks. That nervewracking hush between notes you've forgotten. Our sentence, I guess.

To wonder with all of our might. To remember. We lie here and wait for the light.

p 34 chin music' for Earth

70 Marshall Field's is on fire

p 87 limitless quilt

95 costumes for clothes

102 message?
103 baseball

123 Piersall